NIGHTMERICA

NIGHTMERICA

CORRUPTIONS OF THE AMERICAN DREAM

AMANDA WORTHINGTON

Dragon's Roost Press

Nightmerica: Corruptions of the American Dream is published by Dragon's Roost Press.

This anthology is © 2025 Amanda Worthington and Dragon's Roost Press. Individual stories and poems are © 2025 their respective authors.

Artwork by Lynne Hansen

Printed in the United States of America

Ingram ISBN: 978-1-956824-66-7

Print ISBN: 978-1-956824-68-1

Digital ISBN: 978-1-956824-65-0

Dragon's Roost Press

2470 Hunter Rd.

Brighton, MI 48114

thedragonsroost.biz

No AI was used in the creation of this book.

CONTENTS

PREFACE

AMANDA WORTHINGTON

Like most of us, the American Dream was force-fed to me at an early age. It was the carrot urging me forward, telling me to go to college and marry a respectable man and have well-behaved children and become a homeowner and buy a fancy car and work my hands to the bone, and praise the Lord and save for retirement and place blind faith in that sacred promise of our forefathers—that life, liberty, and the pursuit of happiness were my birthright as an American if I did as I was told.

Well, fuck that noise. I've never been any good at following the rules. I'm a liberal, agnostic woman living in the Bible Belt. Here, churches outnumber schools. Gentrification displaces the hardest-working people in our communities. Children pledge allegiance to a country that values them less than the firearms that might always end their school day early.

I didn't just want to do something. I needed to do something.

It turns out I wasn't alone.

Nightmerica holds no punches. It probably breaks a lot of conventions. Poetry and prose are interwoven. It examines life, liberty, and the pursuit of happiness through the lens of horror and exposes the ways in which the American Dream corrupts our minds, hearts, and bodies. From a newly engaged couple's backwoods struggle for survival to a strange future where captives bear the mental burdens of the ruling class, to a sleep study that isn't what it seems, there is always a price to pay for freedom.

The time of reckoning is upon us. It's time for a greater contribution, one in which a diversity of voices is amplified rather than silenced.

So buckle up—it's going to be a wild ride.

LIFE

THIS PLACE HAS GOOD ROOTS

C.S. MAGNUSON

A small heap of kitchenware littered the sidewalk: pots, pans, tablecloths, a finicky little set of porcelain dishes with a delicate vine pattern.

"Looks like something my grandma had." Jason nudged one of the shattered cups with the toe of his glossy loafer. "Her house was full of shit like this when she passed. Took my parents ages to clean it all out. Why do old people assume we want their crap after they're dead?"

"This one's live enough." Carter folded his thick arms over his chest and nodded to the front door of the house at the far end of the lot. A woman had emerged, flanked by two policemen. "Wiry too. Gotta be at least what? Five six? Five seven? A hundred and twenty pounds soaking wet? I can see why you wanted me here as a bodyguard." He smirked.

"Fuck off," Jason said as Carter snickered. "The company makes me bring someone along for evictions to witness it. It's legal protection for them."

"You can't do this." On the porch, the woman struggled against the officers, twisting in their grasp, doing her best to wrench free. "This is my home. I've never missed a payment. How can they just take your house even if you've paid? It's a crime! The ones who should be arrested are the people at the bank."

A patrol car waited at the curb and just before the group reached it, the woman looked across the lawn and saw Jason standing by the mailbox. Recognition and outrage registered instantly on her face. Jason's shiny suit rendered him out of place in the run-down neighborhood, as if he had *corporate* stamped all over him. "Tell your company this is my home," the woman shrieked. "It's not for sale. My children have roots here. You can't take it from us."

"They always make us out to be the bad guys," Jason said to Carter. "We just buy what the bank puts up for sale. Nothing criminal about it." He shook his head.

All homeowners had to do was follow the rules and play the game right. It wasn't that complicated, but folks never wanted to read the fine print. The system wasn't out to get anyone personally. It was too unfeeling for grudges. When Jason was in a philosophic mood, he liked to think of it as a river. The current was the current, unchanging as far as man was concerned. You could either paddle downstream and let the current help you, or try to paddle upstream, fighting the flow, and eventually it would break you. But as soon as he made that analogy, someone would point out that some people had been born with paddles in hand and others weren't even given a boat. There was always a smart-ass there to ruin the metaphor.

"You breached your contract, ma'am," he called out across the weed-riddled lawn. The grass was halfway up his shins. Didn't the woman ever mow? "The conditions of your mortgage clearly stated you were to keep an active insurance policy on the home at all times. No insurance, no loan, Mrs. Vitale. You signed it, which means you agreed you understood that. The bank was within its rights to foreclose, and Livewell Properties bought the house fair and square. Any issues you have you can take up with the bank. They can explain it to you all over again. They can show you where you signed."

The woman's face turned red as she resisted the arresting officers' attempts to lower her head so they could ease her into the cruiser. "I couldn't get insurance. There are no insurance companies left here."

"That's not my problem, ma'am. It's not Livewell's problem."

"You don't understand. I can't leave. My children have roots here." Her eyes were blazing as she repeated herself, and the arresting officers folded her into the back seat of their vehicle.

"If you want to be mad at someone, be mad at yourself, lady," Jason said though it was unlikely Mrs. Vitale could hear him because the officers had slammed the door shut already.

"I heard that about the insurance companies though," Carter said, showing something like understanding if not sympathy for the woman. "My sister said it's like that in California. After last year's fires, the one company still there pulled out of the state. Here they all left because of the wind storms and tornadoes."

"What'd your sister do?"

"Nothing." Carter shrugged. "She rents so it didn't bother her."

"Yeah, see? I don't get what the big deal is." Jason pressed his foot down on the stalk of a nearby dandelion, mashing the cheery flower between his sole and the earth. "Once Livewell gets this place fixed up, they'll put it up for lease. That woman could turn around and rent the place if she wanted. She could live here without having to worry about maintenance costs or property taxes. It's a win-win."

Livewell only ever improved the neighborhoods they bought into. They would snap up every house on the block they could

C.S. MAGNUSON

get their hands on and fix them up. Before long, there wouldn't be an eyesore on the block. Safety and security would improve, and so would the nearby schools. At least for those who could afford Livewell rents.

"How's Livewell get insurance if there are no companies operating in the state?" Carter frowned, looking like a large but confused child.

"It's different for corporations," Jason explained. "They're insuring *assets*, not homes, and they own the properties outright. If something happens to a house or two, they can absorb the cost because they own a ton, and if something happens on a larger scale, the damages are a write-off at tax time. Like I said: win-win. It's a better deal for everyone."

Jason truly believed that. Home ownership, the core of the supposed American Dream, was an antiquated idea. It tied people down, tethered them to one spot and one community, just like neighborhood schools and all that shit. Flexibility was key in the modern world. Anything less was like eating the same food every day for your entire life or dating the same woman.

The police car rolled away, and Jason moved toward the house. The dandelion he'd been standing on popped back up, only a little worse for wear.

Inside the two-story, nothing had been packed or even reordered. The whole house and all its contents were still in place. Not a moving box in sight. It would take a crew the whole day to bring everything to the curb. But looking beyond Mrs. Vitale's furnishings, Jason could see that the house had good bones and the front rooms at least were tidier than the overgrown yard would lead one to expect. It seemed Mrs. Vitale was a better housekeeper than groundskeeper. It brought Jason a small measure of relief but was tempered by the fact that the house didn't smell great. There was an earthy

6

mustiness pervading the place. "I hope that's not mold," Jason said aloud.

Mold was a deal killer. People hated renting after they heard a house had mold. It was almost as bad as lead pipes. Livewell's crews could cover it up with a coat of paint but if someone's kid started wheezing and it came out that the company knew there had been mold, you could add a couple zeros onto what the payout for medical bills would be. Beyond the living room, inside the kitchen, the door to the basement stood open. Jason decided that would probably explain the smell and if there was mold, hopefully it was contained down there.

Something rattled in that direction and Jason froze, waiting for it to happen again so he could identify it as the clank of a struggling radiator or the protests of an unhappy water heater. Instead, he heard a pinging sound and looked to the windows. Rain had started and was coming down in giant drops that battered the windowpanes like small pebbles. The water washed down the glass and cast a liquid shadow over a small bistro table near the backdoor. It was a table for two at the most. Mrs. Vitale had mentioned having children, but Jason saw no evidence that anyone had lived there with her. Maybe they were grown already. "Hey, Carter?" Jason called.

"Yeah." Carter popped his head in through the front doorway from the porch, a wreath of cigarette smoke like a halo swirling around his shaggy hair.

"I want you to hang here tonight. That woman mentioned kids. They could be adults. Could be mad their mom was evicted. Who knows who has a key. Someone might come back before we can change the locks." This was the stage of the game where former owners got vindictive. Jason had a vision of cement in toilets, holes in drywall, stolen or smashed light fixtures. An angry ex-homeowner—or her enraged older children—could cause tens of thousands of dollars' worth of damage in a few hours if they wanted to. Some people would rather sink the boat than watch someone else sail off in it without them. "People can be so petty," Carter sniffed.

A few hours later, Jason woke in his armchair in front of the television to a flash of lightning so bright he was instantly reminded of snow. For a split second, it was as if a heavy winter layer of frost had settled over everything in his apartment. He wriggled in his sweatshirt, fighting off a chill brought on by the idea of cold rather than an actual drop in temperature. When thunder cracked and his phone rang in his lap at the same time, he jumped and nearly knocked the device to the floor.

"Hey, it's Pat down at the station," a voice said as soon as he answered. "I thought you'd want to know that Mrs. Vitale has been released from custody."

Fighting off the sleepiness that still clung to him, Jason leaned forward in his chair. "Why?"

"Why did I think you'd want to know?"

"No, why was she let go?"

"No room in the inn, I'm afraid. We're short on cells 'til they build the new jail. We've got to pick and choose who goes and who stays. Murderers and gang bangers, folks who want to beat up their wives trump irate ex-homeowners."

"No. No." Jason stood, the leather club chair releasing his body with a squelch. "Can't you do me a favor on this, Pat?"

"I did. I called you to let you know she's out. That's the favor."

"Fuck." Jason hung up and immediately dialed Carter. He needed a heads-up that Mrs. Vitale could be heading his way, but the man's phone rang with no answer. "Fuck," Carter must have bounced.

The power was out when he arrived at the house. That whole side of the block was dark, and the houses were menacing blocks, granite-gray against an angry navy sky. Pulling into the driveway, Jason fumbled in his console for the garage door remote—he'd picked it up off Mrs. Vitale's countertop before leaving earlier that afternoon and hoped he could avoid a dousing, as the rain was coming down harder than before. No such luck. As the door rose, his headlights illuminated the interior. It was packed full of junk, leaving no room to park a car —not a little sedan let alone an enormous SUV like Jason drove.

"Guess we'll just consider this a stress test," he grumbled, taking a stab at looking on the bright side.

But there was no upside to the cramped and cluttered garage.In the headlight's beams, Jason could see bags and bags of fertilizer, insecticides, and old paint cans. He couldn't just throw this stuff into the garbage bin. It would need to be disposed of at a hazardous waste dump site. Yet another errand and hiccup Jason could add to the list of hiccups this house had presented him with.

Pulling his jacket over his head like a hood, he managed to keep his hair and clothes mostly dry as he dashed up the driveway. His wet shoes on the smooth concrete of the garage floor were like ice skates and he almost wiped out as soon as he stepped inside. He flailed his arms, trying to regain his balance, and lost his grip on his cell phone. It landed a couple yards away with a crack and the flashlight went out. "Dammit, Carter." If the man had followed instructions and stayed put, Jason would be at home still, dry, drinking a beer, and maybe finishing off a plate of left-over Chinese food.

The garage was a maze in the dark. Making his way to the door into the house in pitch blackness, he tripped over a jumble of garden tools, their long handles like a mess of jumbo pick-up sticks. Again, he avoided taking a spill, catching himself on the banister, a rickety old thing that deposited a splinter the size of a toothpick deep into Jason's palm.

"I will murder you, Carter," he vowed but stopped on the wooden steps leading up into the kitchen. A shape by the street had caught his eye. The lamp was out but the form alongside the curb was familiar. It was Carter's car. "You have got to be kidding me," he growled entering the house. "I swear, if I drove all this way because you fell asleep and didn't answer your phone...Carter? Where're you at?"

Standing just inside the kitchen, he cocked his head, listening for a reply from somewhere in the house. All he heard was the sound of the rain on the windows and the trickling noise it made sweeping down the gutters. "Carter?"

His hand throbbed but he felt his way to the sink, hoping maybe Mrs. Vitale had kept a flashlight underneath it. Opening the cabinet door released a fetid burst of mildewy air that made him gag, but he groped around in the clammy void until he felt something that could be a camping lantern.. He flicked it on and got a better look at where he'd been reaching moments earlier. At the back of the cabinet, the drywall had been torn away, revealing the wall cavity and the space between the studs —something else that would need to be fixed.

Jason leaned in closer, checking the pipes for rust and leaks. Around each of the joins, tiny hairs protruded. He exhaled an irritated sigh, and the thin strands quivered. Jason pinched a couple off and examined them. Roots. The strands were roots. And there were more of them hanging down inside the wall, a cascade of fine white filaments. "Shit." Jason felt his hopes of an easy turn-around for the house sink. If roots had invaded the walls that extensively, they could be in the exterior sewer line or even in the water line. That might mean a complete excavation and re-pipe. It certainly meant time and money.

Jason stood but failed to clear the cabinet and hit the back of his head. He didn't see stars, but he did notice the multitude of stupid, hanging macramé plant holders dangling in every corner of the room for the first time. There were hanging plants galore —pothos and pictus, long ivy, he guessed. Jason had a girlfriend once who was a plant enthusiast and he remembered some of the names, though he wouldn't have been able to tell them apart.

Vines and tendrils dripped from the pots, dangling like limp insect legs, swaying gently in a breeze Jason couldn't feel. Some of the climbing plants had sent out runners. The runners had attached to the walls with tiny aerial roots that embedded themselves in the drywall. Jason swept the lantern's beam around the room, taking in the degree of growth. The vines extended along the top of the wall like a decorative border or bunting that ran from corner to corner. They dripped low enough that they hit the floor and crept out toward the center of the room.

In the shadowy corner where the cabinets ended and the breakfast nook began, a tuft of gray caught Jason's eye. He aimed the lantern in that direction. A mouse had gotten caught in the vines. With a knot of green tendrils around its belly, Jason guessed it must have got stuck and struggled, its thrashing only tangling it further until it finally strangled. The mouse was dead, already completely desiccated, its once beady eyes now crusty little pits, all moisture sucked from its furry hide. It was gross, but Jason had seen worse than a single dead mouse in some of the houses Livewell purchased.

He stuck his head out the kitchen door into the living room, expecting to find Carter there snoozing on the couch with his feet on the coffee table. The TV was on but there was no sign of him. "Yo, Carter!" Jason's voice echoed in the old house. "I've been calling you, man." A cellphone sat on the coffee table beside a can of Coors. "Where are you?"

There was a base funk to the air that smelled vaguely biological, and Jason shined his flashlight down a hallway that led off the living room to the bathroom among other rooms. "Dude. You reek. You know there are pills you can take if you want to keep eating bean burritos without creating a biohazard." He headed down the passage, flashlight in hand. It took him a moment to realize that what he had thought was patterned wallpaper at the far end was actually more plants covering the walls. He knocked on the bathroom door and pushed it open when there was no answer.

Carter wasn't there. Just more plants. Mrs. Vitale was obsessed. Jason shook his head. The woman had let them run wild, almost taking over the small powder room. He tugged angrily at one of the vines, but the suckers had burrowed deep, and a small chunk of drywall came with it as he pulled it away. "You've got to be kidding me." The plant aesthetic was one thing. Turning the place into a jungle and letting the greenery destroy the house was another.

The lights came back on with a flicker as he stood there holding the vine. His reflection in the mirror above the sink startled him backward and he grabbed the back of the toilet to steady himself, noticing a smear of red when he removed his hand. His palm was bleeding and the splinter from the banister was still embedded there. Jason winced, yanked it free, and turned on the tap to rinse off the blood. The pipes groaned but failed to produce any water. "Oh, no."

It was just as he had feared. Worse even. The pipes were shot—clogged with roots. With the light on, Jason could see them sprouting from the tap. In fact, they seemed to be getting longer as he watched. Very slowly, they stretched and extended beyond the brass sink fixture, reaching downward toward the drain. No, not the drain. Toward Jason's hand which still hovered in the basin, oozing blood from the splinter's gash.

Unnerved, Jason jerked his hand back, cradling it protectively against his chest, not even minding that he leaked blood on his shirt. Slowly, he backed out of the room and into the hallway. Opposite the bathroom was another room. The county records called it a fourth bedroom. In the listing the marketing team created, Livewell would call it a "generous ground-floor bedroom with office potential." It wasn't being used for either purpose at the moment. The room held no furniture, just bags and bags of fertilizer. It spilled out of bags and buckets used for transporting it, staining the wooden floors. It explained the stench though.

Jason pulled his shirt up over his face to offset the smell and moved back down the hallway toward the stairs. "Carter?" he called from the bottom step, a rising sense of unease making his voice shake and his legs feel overly supple.

With increased anxiety weighing him down, it took him twice as long as it normally would have to reach the landing at the stairs' midway point, and there he froze. More drywall had been torn away—whole sheets of it—and inside the walls he could see roots as thick as baseball bats growing from the lower floor all the way up to the very top of the house. They were pale with little green shoots, and eyes like tubers had. *Eyes.* They really did look like eyes. Hundreds of tiny peepers watched Jason as he ascended the stairs. He took another step or two before a thump and a moan echoed up the stairwell from the lower floor. "Carter? Is that you?" Glad to have a reason to move away from those staring roots, Jason hurried back down the stairs.

There was still no sign of Carter in the living room or in the kitchen but, the basement door was open. Jason aimed his lantern down the long flight of stairs to the concrete floor below, certain the groan had come from there.

It didn't look right, the floor. It wasn't smooth the way it should have been. It looked like someone had dumped a box of rope and cables there and hadn't bothered to pick them up again. The ropes moved, writhing and twisting, and Jason's frazzled mind screamed *snakes*. But they weren't snakes. They were vines. Fat ones. Or worse than fat. These were *muscular*-looking vines, though Jason knew it was strange to describe plants that way.

"Jay, is that you?" Carter's voice, reedy and quavering, floated up from the basement.

Jason sagged against the doorway. "It's me, bud. Come on up and let's get outta here. Call it a day, huh?" He'd come back in the morning with a gallon of Weed-Begone. Five gallons maybe. Whatever the largest quantity it came in was.

"I can't move, Jay," Carter called. "I'm stuck."

"Stuck how?" Jason's mind went to a thousand different places at once, none of which were the basement. "On what?"

"I fell, man. I fell and I need help."

"What about the plants?"

"I think I can walk if someone would just help me up."

"What about the fucking plants, Carter?"

"The plants?" Carter sounded confused. "There are plants, but I don't know, man. They're just plants."

"They're not...moving?" Jason stared at the vines at the base of the stairs. They were motionless. Only their shadows shifted slightly as the hanging bulb over the stairs swayed slightly.

"They're plants, Jason. Why would they move?"

Jason took a deep breath. "I'm coming down then, Carter. But we're leaving, okay? Like right away."

"Whatever you say."

Keeping a tight grip on the railing, Jason crept down the stairs until he could finally see Carter on the floor across the room. The burly man's torso was wrapped so tightly in vines that it looked as though it was squeezed in half. His face was purple and his eyes bloodshot.

Jason didn't know how he could possibly still be alive after being constricted like that, but he had just heard his voice. "Carter, man, what…how're you..?"

The vines around Carter tightened and his tongue popped from his mouth. It waved in the air, long and green and glossy. He raised his head. Blood dribbled from his mouth, and Jason saw that the thing sticking out of Carter's mouth wasn't his tongue at all. A vine extended up from the spool of green wrapped around his middle and disappeared into his neck. It had stabbed through the tender flesh at the base of the trachea and traveled up through his throat to his mouth where it functioned as a tongue. "Help me up, man." The voice was wet and garbled.

Jason screamed and turned to run, but something wrapped around his ankle, and he was falling. He landed hard at the base of the stairs, unable to breathe. Vines rippled beneath his back. They moved around him, cradling him, but before they could pin him down entirely, he sat up. His hands still free, he tore at the plants around him, ripping their leaves off in shreds. The plants cried out, sounding like injured children. The sound caught him off guard, but he didn't stop. He continued to assault the vines that were doing their best to wrap him up in a cocoon like the one that had ensnared Carter.

He freed his ankles and fought back the creepers that reached for his hips and thighs until he was able to stand. On a shelf near the base of the stairs was a candle and a box of matches. Jason grabbed the box and opened it with shaking hands, spilling most of the matches on the floor but managing to light one. He flicked it into the center of the largest clump of foliage by his feet, and then lit another.

The plants screamed. A hundred tiny wheezing voices cried out. And several deeper voices too. "Stop! Stop, please. It hurts."

Startled, Jason looked to the corner of the basement. There, huddled in the corner, were three naked children. Their skin was green as emeralds, and they looked up at Jason with milky-jade eyes. A solid mass of leaves and knotted vines grew behind them, stalks sprouting from cracks in the basement walls, vines like umbilical cords tethering the children to the heart of the growth.

"Mama, make him stop," the three children howled.

Jason turned to see Mrs. Vitale behind him with a shovel. She brought it down on his head with force. Jason's legs turned to water, his spine to butter. He sank to the floor.

"I told you this was our home." Mrs. Vitale raised the shovel once more, this time directly over Jason's face. "You wouldn't listen. I could never let some corporation take that from me, from *them*." She nodded to the three chlorophyll-rich youths across the room. "My children have roots here, and roots must be nurtured."

NATURAL SELECTION

DAN B. FIERCE

"My God! It's so beautiful up here." The hike wasn't the only thing taking Marcus's breath away. The ascent up the Colorado mountain proved how underprepared they had both been for this rugged trail. "Wow. I should get a 360 of this."

Marcus scanned the view in a panorama with his phone's camera, starting with his partner Alexander and completing a full circle. Only, Alexander wasn't standing when he came back around; he was kneeling on one leg, a hand extended, a gorgeous ring in an open box in one hand. Marcus almost dropped his phone after what was happening had sunk in. At this moment, his breathing had caught for an entirely different reason.

Alexander peered up at his lover through altitude-slowed breaths with big, brown, puppy dog eyes glistening in hopeful anticipation. "Marcus Overstreet, we've accomplished so much together, made each other laugh, loved, and lived as partners. I want to share the rest of my life with you. I hope you feel the same. Will you marry me?"

"Yes!" Tears streamed down Marcus's face. Had the temperature been a few degrees colder, they may have frozen in place. "Oh. My. God! A thousand times yes!" He couldn't contain his excitement as Alex slipped the ring on his finger.

The sun glinted on the carefully mounted rock at the center of the thin white gold band, dwarfing the two others ton either side. There weren't many times that Marcus had ever been caught speechless, but this one certainly qualified. Alexander stood, taking his lover's hands in his. They embraced deeply, Marcus still vibrating with excitement. They broke their hug, kissing with a passion usually reserved for more private quarters. The lip-lock ceased. They simply held each other at the pinnacle of the mountain, swaying to music no one could else hear.

After their hearts had calmed down, Marcus broke away, swiping at the moisture on his cheeks. "You hooker. Why didn't you tell me this was what we were coming up here for?"

"Surprise?"

"And then some." Marcus admired his new jewelry, glowing brighter than the diamond atop his finger. He stopped looking at it and placed an accusatory hand on his hip. "You ruined my 360 shot." Once again, he raised his phone, reactivating the camera. "Selfie first." He stood next to his new fiancée, making sure to snap the picture with his right hand so that the one with the diamonds on it would show. He took one of them with the valley behind them, as well as one of them kissing. He double-checked the shots, ecstatic with the results. "Oh, that's going up on Scrapbook for sure." He broke from his future husband to finally take the shot he thought he wanted. "Now hold still. I'm starting and ending with you." He began his panoramic image, spinning a full circle. When he returned to Alexander, they were no longer alone. Marcus screamed in surprise at the screen.

Alexander's eyes got as big as boulders. "What's behind me?"

A slow clap echoed over the mountaintop. Alex turned to the source. It was joined by another set of hands and another. There were three of them. Each man had a rifle slung over his shoulder and a large, menacing Arkansas toothpick sheathed at his side. They were dressed head to toe in camouflage, faces painted to match. Two of them, the younger-looking ones, smirked in a way that made the Marcus uncomfortable. The older one, age and dubious genetics outing him as a blood relative grinned with what Marcus would have called summer teeth. "Summer there, summer missing," he would explain as they both giggled at the joke. The grin facing them now, more like a pined grimace, didn't make him feel much like a hearty belly laugh, and he was sure Alex shared is concern.

"Ain't this a sight?" The older one turned his head back to the camo-faced boys, his drawl placing him firmly in the not-from-around-here category.

"Shore is, Pa," answered one of the kids, looking to be in his late teens. A small spill of blond hair fell over his forehead from under an excessively worn cap, obviously his favorite.

"Hope we didn't ruin your special moment." The patriarch spat a glob of tobacco juice on the ground.

Marcus winced in disgust at the brown puddle, shrinking back almost instinctively to Alexander's side. "Is there something we can help you with?"

The older man's brow furrowed for a few seconds before softening to that stained and gap-toothed grin again. "Naw. We's just been out a-huntin'. Ain't that right, boys?" He spat another glob, this time a bit more off to the side.

The darker-haired, older kid spoke as he fiddled with his hunting knife. "Yep. Just mindin' our own business, and we come upon y'all."

Marcus caught Alexander's eyes darting around, looking for the nearest path the would guide them away from the newcomers. "Well, we'll just leave you to it then. Happy hunting." Alex was clearly on full alert despite his offhand remark. his reassuring hand on Marsus's lower bock conveyed his sense of urgency.

"Isn't hunting animals in state parks illegal?" Marcus thought he said it low enough to prevent the hunters from hearing.

"Where the hell did you learn to whisper?' Alexander grunted through gritted teeth. "In a helicopter?"

"Never said we was huntin'... animals." The patriarch glowered at the couple, now paused in their retreat. "Didn't mean to disturb ya none."

"Good luck." Alex feigned a smile, quickening their previous pace, likely because he was afraid Marcus would rattle off something that would get the trio's complete attention. Getting a little more forceful, he grabbed Marcus' shoulders, aiming him away from the newcomers.

"Good luck to you too." The man scoured the rapidly blossoming clouds. "Looks like you'll be needing it. See you, boys, real soon." Another puddle of chaw hit the rocks as a sneer overcame the man's face. The boys joined behind him, watching intensely as the couple beat a hasty retreat.

Alexander and Marcus made the Sawtooth traverse easily enough, putting as much space as they could between the hillbillies and themselves. Still, the sparsely spaced cairns marking the trail down the opposite mountain made the best route challenging to discern. Angry clouds above burst out a tantrum of a storm. The ground became muddy surrounding the willows, and loose dirt and scree hindered their progress.

Unable to bear the silence any longer, Marcus huffed. "How much longer do we have?"

"I'd say, at this pace, likely another hour or two. The descent will be a lot easier and faster. I promise."

"That's because you're planning on pushing me off a cliff, aren't you?"

Alexander finally smiled. "Only if you don't move your cute ass." He swatted Marcus squarely on the tush. Marcus giggled like a schoolgirl as Alexander found the main trail. "Over there. Another marker."

"You go ahead of me," Marcus said. "That way, you can clear the spider webs.

"Gee, thanks."

"I love you." Marcus indicated all of the surroundings. "This? Not so much."

They kept their footing until they reached the tree line once again. Marcus's feet and knees ached, and they were both drenched from the downpour. But the adrenaline from the encounter kept his mind on task.

"At least we'll have some cover from the rain now." Alexander stopped on a rock outcropping to rest.

Marcus sat next to him, huffing in the increased oxygen levels in grateful lungfuls. "Do you think they followed us?"

"Not sure." Alexander huffed in short spurts. "Didn't hear anything, but if they're experienced hunters, they know how not to be heard." He checked his watch. "It's noon. We'd better get moving. This mountain is more complicated."

"Fan-fucking-tastic." Marcus paused. "You'd better be happy that I love you. I don't put up with bugs and weather for just anyone."

"Unless there's a shoe sale involved."

Marcus faked a shocked expression. "Bitch."

Alexander chuckled. The laughter hung in the thin air like a specter before evaporating in the wind. "I knew that I wanted to bring you up here to propose. I've had a lot of good memories here with my family. Now I have one more."

Marcus looked at his ring again. "It's a damned good thing you did." He held it up, admiring the jewels and sparkling metal.

"I'm sorry the moment got ruined." He hesitated, taking in his lover's expression as he gushed over his new ring. "Let's go. Remember, tomorrow it's your turn to torture me."

"If you play your cards right, we can start the torture tonight." Marcus gave his best seductive grin. "

So... You singing along to *The Sound of Music?*"

"You know, it's not too late to get a room with *two* beds," this elicited a full guffaw from Alexander. Thunder crashed as another storm flashed to life over the peak to their backs, causing Marcus to emit a yelp of surprise.

"We should look for someplace to hole up. These storms don't last very long, but they can drop a lot of water, and lightning can be hazardous here. This area isn't a very well patrolled part of the park."

Marcus sighed. "Just get me home, Bear Grylls. I'm over it." They both laughed as they got to their feet, wincing.

They followed the trail as best they could deeper into the willows, but the markings were sparse. Finding the correct pathway proved to be more of a challenge than the Sawtooth behind them. Once again, the cairns marking the right path were practically nonexistent.

Alexander checked his phone. "Shit. Still no service."

"What the hell do you need service for? Don't you know where you're going?" Marcus did nothing to disguise the frustration in his voice.

Alexander glared at Marcus. "I know you're not having fun, but that isn't helping."

A twig snapped on the trail behind them. Both men swung their gaze toward the sound but could make out nothing. Another clap of thunder rumbled as the first few raindrops made it past the tree canopy.

"Let's go." Alex held out a hand to his fiancée, his face a blanket of concern, his stare unwavering from the direction of the sound. "Now."

"Did you see something? You're scaring me."

"No, but I don't want to see what made that sound. I also don't want to get much wetter. We need to hurry up and find someplace to sit this out."

Alexander looked around rapidly for a marker of any kind. His eye found a pyramid of stones down the hill from where they were. Leading the way, he found footing amid the slippery pine needles, carefully guiding them both down the steep grade of the hillside to the marker. Stepping over fallen trees and around the dwarf willows and bramble bushes, they made it to the cairn as the sky opened up, dumping its payload upon them in sheets.

Lightning struck a tree twenty or so feet behind them, toppling the upper half to the ground with a calamitous crash. A fire ignited from the strike.

"Fuck!" Alexander rushed back up the hill to douse the flames.

Marcus saw his betrothed heading back the way they came. "What the hell are you doing?"

"If these pine needles catch fire, we'll never outrun the flames. Help me put it out."

They worked in tandem to extinguish the immediate danger the felled part presented, but the rest of the tree had been split and still burned. Without a saw to bring the tree down, all they could do was hope that the rain gave them a head start. A crackle, snap, and brushy thump dashed that thought as a flaming branch found the dried carpet of needles.

"Go! Go now." Veins bulged from Alexander's neck as panic set in. His steps got sloppy as he hurried Marcus downhill. "There. Another cairn." He pointed to another stack of pebbles atop a small outcropping of granite-gray moss-covered stones.

Behind them, the flames licked at the trunk of another tree. Soon, it, too, was engulfed. The chain ignited the forest as the men scrambled. Finally, the sky loosed a deluge, drowning the majority of the conflagration.

"Over here!" In the torrent and smoke, all they could make out was a silhouette, a man signaling them from down the hill. "This way. There's a cabin!"

The couple glanced at each other, unsure of the invitation. "Who is it? Is it one of those rednecks?"

"I'm not sure." Alexander placed a hand over his eyes to shield them from the downpour. "I don't think so. His voice sounds different."

Whoever it was had longer hair, tied up in a top knot, but Marcus couldn't make out any other details. They both decided that getting out of the storm would be in their better interest. Just as the pair reached the last ten feet, Alexander looked up to see a moss-covered and very dilapidated cabin. It had been so overgrown that it blended with the scenery, but the weather-rusted roof looked as if it would at least keep them somewhat dry.

Alexander never took his eyes off the man. Marcus was a little worried that the figure ahead of them might be some sort of mirage. Neither of them saw the smooth granite rock glinting in the path, and Alex stepped directly onto it. The mud-caked sole of his hiking boot hit the slick, wet surface of the smooth stone, and over he went. His ankle snapped audibly, collapsing him like a sack of potatoes, and he struck his head on the stump of a rotted tree.

Marcus rushed to his side. "Oh, my Gawd! Baby! Are you okay?"

"Yeah. I don't think so."

Alexander's head was bleeding, and his foot was twisted in a way Marcus didn't think it was supposed to twist. The man who had signaled them clambered up the hill to help. He dropped to his knees next to Alexander to inspect the injured ankle.

Marcus held Alexander's hand. The stranger was a good-looking man, muscular and rugged with long brown hair tied up in a man-bun at the peak of his skull. But even the man's handsome features didn't set Marcus at ease. He was too unkempt, his body filthy, and his clothes tattered. What was thought to be a tan at first now looked like a thick layer of dirt. *Maybe he's homeless*, Marcus felt a pang of shame for his suspicions.

"Give me a hand. Help me lift him up on one, two..." the stranger and Marcus pulled Alexander painfully to his feet. Their patient yelped as the slightest amount of weight settled onto his injury.

Marcus took the uninjured side, and their new friend helped with keeping pressure off the twisted ankle. Twenty feet felt like twenty miles on the uneven way to the cabin, and rain-slicked boulders slowed progress even more. They finally made it to a slight stretch of flat land, which served as a stoop for the house. A tattoo peeked out from under the stranger's ragged, long sleeve when he reached for the door. It appeared to be a swastika. Marcus pursed his lips, checking to see whether Alexander had noticed it, too, but his future hubby had clamped his eyes shut, likely from pain.

"Careful. That board is rotted." The man guided Alexander away from it as he saw Marcus looking at his ink, and yanked his cuff down defiantly.

Marcus stopped dead on the stoop, wrestling with the decision to enter. Alexander released a yowl of pain that convinced him to step in.

The man glowered at the pair as he led them inside the structure, then a smile softened his features. "It's okay, man. I understand. Tattoos tend to catch people off-guard if they see them. I'm Tim."

The air was musty inside the cabin, reeking of dirt, rot, and mold, but it was reasonably dry. They sat Alexander on a makeshift stool fashioned from a two-foot-high piece of a tree trunk. He winced in agony, a jolt of electric pain reminding him of the obvious. "Well, Tim, I am certainly glad to meet you." Alex shot an accusatory glance at Marcus, who shook his head. Alexander punctuated his silent suggestion, causing Marcus to slump in defeat.

"Thank you for your help, Tim. I apologize for my 'stranger danger' ways." Marcus walked over to the fireplace, the carved figure on the mantle sent a shiver down his spine. "I tend to be more cautious when I'm feeling vulnerable. Bad memories." He turned back toward their savior as he spoke. "Are you all by your-"

Tim walloped Marcus with a right hook, dropping him to the ground. The look in his eye was far less welcoming now; it was maniacal, unhinged. He kicked the fallen man hard in the ribs, launching him briefly off the ground with the force of the blow. "I guess you should have listened to your instincts." Rolling up his sleeve, he revealed what Marcus had thought he'd seen: a swastika. Tim threw another punch that landed hard in Marcus' left eye. "I hate people like you." Alexander started to get up from the stump, but their host kicked his bad foot out from under him, sending him crashing to the floor in a new starburst of intense pain.

Marcus screamed, blood pooling in his mouth and flowing in a thick stream from his swelling lips. "Somebody help! Help us!"

Tim sneered with sadistic delight. "No one's going to hear you out here. They were all smart and got off of the mountain." He feigned another blow, causing Marcus to flinch and throw his hands up to protect himself. Their host uttered a guttural laugh. "I guess I can do a bit of the Lord's work tonight and rid the world of a couple of fags. It will be weeks before they find your bodies. Hell, maybe I'll find you myself. I'll be seen as a hero for giving your families closure." He leaned down to face Alexander, placing a boot on his victim's broken ankle. "That's if they want anything to do with you abominations." He stood back upright, looking around, scheming. "Got to make it seem like an accident or that you turned on each other."

Marcus yelled again. "Help! Anyone? Help us, please." Tears streamed down the right side of his face; his left eye had already swollen shut. His pleas diminished within seconds as reality set in.

"Keep it up. As I said, no one can hear you." Despite his assurances of solitude, Tim still had an air of impatience, as if he wanted to be done with the business. "Hmm... How to make it look like you both hurt yourself and died in here."

"You'll never get away with it." Alexander crawled over to his partner, shielding him from their assailant.

Tim bent down again, a crazed look in his eye. "That was cheesy. You write that yourself? I thought you gays hated clichés. I thought all of you gays were the creative types, all arts and crafts and glittery shit." He stood back, looking at the men clutching each other. He gazed upon them as an artist would a blank canvas. He held his chin in his hand in contemplation. "You know what? I do some arts and crafts, too. Yeah, I know, surprising. Here. Let me show you."

Tim rifled through a shoebox, producing a pair of makeshift gloves ending in a splay of five menacing claws. "I got this from watching that TV show, *Grimm*. I thought, 'Now that's ingenious. Make my kills look like an animal did it.' Around here, nobody would question it if someone got attacked by a bear. I have one for a wolf's teeth and claws too."

He approached the pair marveling over his creation as he donned them, much like Marcus had admired his ring. "Since there's two of you, I think a bear attack might be in order. What do you say?" He shot a hand out to Alexander's face, placing just enough pressure on the sharp ends to cause five little trickles of blood to bloom. "It's the right season for bear cubs. Plenty of them around. Real cute, too. Do you know what happens when a hiker gets too close? Pulls in real close to get just the right picture to show all of his little homo friends? He runs into mama bear. Yeah, a mama bear'd make a nice pile of hamburger out of two pretty boys like you."

Alexander spat at him. "A mama bear with size ten Timberlands? He nodded at the muck-caked boots. "You'll get caught eventually."

"Why are you doing this?" Marcus struggled to a sitting position. "We didn't do anything to you."

"You're gays," Tim stated. "That's bad enough." He kneeled, pointing the claw at them. "Let me tell you a story. I joined the military to go over to Afghanistan. Went over to protect this country from those jihadi Al Qaeda bastards. I'm fighting for the good ol' U. S. of A – apple pie and Superman and shit—but by the time I got back, this whole country had been 'pussified' by all of the political correctness crap and you freaks. Half of these granola chewing dipshits that come around here stroll around like they are all high and mighty, telling the whole country to take it easy on their feelings. Safe spaces, my ass. No one was worried about my feelings when I had mortar shells dropped by the Taliban or was dodging mines set in the roads. I lost some of my best friends over there in that desert. And for what? To come back to this shit?"

He swung the claw, gashing Alexander across the chest, shredding shirt and skin alike. Marcus screamed, frantically trying to help as blood began to pour out of the wounds.

Tim continued, as emotionless as a man reading a bedtime story. "So, I get back to the states after they let me go. For four years, I was there. Three tours. Then I get out—"

"Let me guess," growled Marcus defiantly, "dishonorable discharge for psychotic conduct?"

Tim's eyes shone unhinged. Again, their assailant slashed, this time opening fresh wounds down Marcus' arm. His victim yowled in agony as he continued his story as if nothing had happened. "Something like that. I lost all of my benefits. My military brothers get to be buried in Arlington. I won't even get that honor when I die. People would have thanked me for my service almost every day." Tim was practically frothing at the mouth, spittle flinging out in streamers. "What the hell do they thank you for? Forcing them to bake you a cake? This country has lost its way, and it's because of people like you."

Alexander sat up gingerly, blood seeping through his fingers where the weapon slashed him. "You blame us for you getting booted out of the services? They probably saw you for the Nazi scum you are."

"Ah, good. You can sit up." Tim reared back with the claw again, causing a satisfying wince from both victims. He dropped his hand to his side, the dull black symbol of hate glaring at his prey from under the falling sleeve. "Let's make this more interesting. Up!" he shouted. "On your feet, ladies." He heaved Marcus upright, motioning for him to grab his partner, do-si-do. "We'll go outside, you boys can run, and when I catch you, I'll kill you. Just like the real thing. Okay?"

Alexander became dead weight, refusing to budge. He grimaced in red hot hatred at their tormentor. "Fuck you. We're not going anywhere."

"Damn." He released his captive, watching with glee as he crumpled back to the floor in a heap. "That's a shame. I liked this cabin, too. Guess I'll have to rip the door off of its hinges to make it convincing." Tim paced the floor as he formulated his plan. "I'll give you boys this much. You gave me a lot more trouble than the last gal did. She was a lot of fun. Out here hiking by herself. She talked all kinds of tough with her cornpone accent, but she had her own bear attack in the end. She was a pretty little toe-headed blonde. I have to say this thing is becoming my favorite. Not too big. Not too small. Just right."

Tim reared up with the claw. Alexander held his arms up in protection as Marcus screamed. A shot pierced the air. Crimson blossomed in the front of Tim's tattered and already filthy shirt. He looked down at it in disbelief before dropping to his knees and then to the cabin floor. Behind him, with smoke wafting out of the barrel of his rifle, was the elder hunter they had met on the mountaintop, flanked still by the younger men. He spat tobacco as he lowered his gun. The three approached, keeping a watchful eye and weapons trained on the wounded man. Tim twitched as his essence pumped out of his body with each decreasing heartbeat.

"I told you it weren't no bear what took out Jenny." He accentuated his words with another punt to Tim's ribcage, a splatter of used tobacco staining the dying man's face. "I seen plenty of animal attacks. I knew that ain't what happened to my baby sister." One final stiff kick rocked the unmoving madman. "Nobody messes with my kinfolk and gets away with it." Tim gurgled one last time, and his body stopped moving. After a few moments, the country man's knife-like stares softened as he held out a hand to Alexander. One of his companions mimicked the action. "Come on. We got to get you boys to help."

Alexander scuttled backward, dragging Marcus with him. "How do we know you aren't going to hurt us?"

"Us?" scoffed the elder man incredulously. "We don't mean you no harm."

With a grunt of effort, the more talkative of the boys added, "Our uncle has hisself a husband. Just went to the wedding last year."

"Sure was one helluva party. Whole family was there." The man pulled Alexander gingerly to standing. "Easy now. Gimme your weight. There you are." The group started hobbling the injured men out of the cabin. Alexander began sobbing as he was led back onto the trail. "Whoa, now. What's with the waterworks?"

"I feel horrible." Alexander wept as they limped along, barely able to see the ground through the cascade of feelings. "I'm sorry. I'm so sorry I misjudged you."

"We both did," croaked Marcus through strained vocal cords. "We don't even know your names."

The hillbillies almost laughed in unison, their jocularity easing the newly engaged couple's minds just a bit. "Name's Jim, but most people call me 'Papa Moonshine' on account of my still back home. These are my boys, Jim Junior-"

"You can call me JJ," piped the blonde.

"-And the other is Jacob."

"Paw, you know I prefer..." He trailed off, focused on something in front of them.

The whole party stopped in their tracks, following the boy's gaze to a clearing in the trail below. The parking lot was a few thousand feet beyond that, but it may as well have been a million miles away. A pair of black bear cubs frolicked in the tall grass between the group and their goal. They all stood still, watching the babies play until a wind blew and changed the animals' demeanor.

"Why don't we just go around them?" Marcus looked baffled at the predicament.

"Quiet." The cubs both stood on their haunches, peering around until they found the group. Jim's eyes grew concerned. "Their momma cain't be far off." Jim craned his neck as far as he could both ways before slowly turning Alexander around with him.

"What's going on?" Alexander straightened as best he could, twisting alongside his savior.

"I said shut up." He narrowed his gaze, leering to the top of the mountain, listening for steps, cracking twigs, or anything to give away the mother bear's location. His eyes locked at a shadowy patch moving over a rock outcropping fifty yards away. Slowly, he started to return Alexander to the ground, his eyes remaining trained on the animal. "Gonna have to put you down for a bit. Keep an eye out, boys. I gotta reload."

"You can't—"

"It comes down to her or us; I might have to." Jim interrupted. "I don't wanna do it. She's got young 'uns, too. But I ain't come this far to avenge one family member only to bury more." He loaded a few more shells into the chamber. "Let's try to work around her. Slow-like. Jake, grab up this 'un here and start down. Work sideways away from the babies so that momma sees we ain't no threat. Slow. I'll keep watch."

The boys led the injured men away, their father trailing carefully behind, his back to them, prepared if the momma grew impatient. They had just made a wide berth of the frolicking furballs when a gunshot echoed through the valley. Jim whirled, yowling in pain, clutching his right shoulder and almost dropping his rifle. "Son of a bitch!"

The men looked to the hill above them. There stood Tim. Blue smoke wafted from the point of the pistol as the psychotic man leered down at them. "How does it feel, you inbred redneck?" He aimed again with the gun. "It's not my preferred way of doing things, but in a pinch, it'll do just fine." He cocked the hammer back as he stepped forward for a closer target.

"You hadn't oughta done that."

"Shoulder for a shoulder. Any last words before I put you out of your misery?"

"Nah." Jim stood. "I reckon she'll do the talking just fine."

Tim's eyes grew wide as hot air hit the back of his neck. Slowly, he turned around, barely getting a scream out before a claw swiped down across his body, gashing his face and diagonally across his chest. The gun flew from his hand as he fell, clattering on a cluster of moss-covered stones. The cubs beat a hasty retreat opposite the group of humans that had piqued their curiosity.

They ambled uphill past their enraged and protective mother and the victim she was tearing into with such vengeance.

Jim watched for a moment; then, he returned his attention to the others. "Let's git while we can. Before a Ranger shows up and starts askin' a lot of questions." They made their way to the parking lot just as the sun brought the shadow of the mountain upon them.

As medics tended to the injured men in the parking lot, a bruised and battered Alexander and Marcus looked up at the mountain trail. There were beasts in those woods–human and animal. That much was certain. If not for hope, those things couldn't have been overcome.

Sitting on the tail of the ambulance while holding an ice pack on his swollen eye, Marcus chimed, "I get to pick the next vacation."

From the gurney loaded in the back, Alexander struggled to lift his head enough to see his love. "That's fair."

MRS. MERRIWEATHER'S LACTATION SERVICES

K.M. BENNETT

"Hello. Aileen, I take it?" A tall woman with a fashionable gray bob hairstyle extended her hand for a shake. She wore a pressed gray pantsuit with pale pink pinstripes. Wrinkles resembling parentheses surrounded her thin lips as she cracked a wide smile.

"That's me."

"I'm Mrs. Merriweather, certified lactation consultant. I hear we're having some problems with breastfeeding?"

"Yeah. She didn't make her birth weight at two weeks, so the pediatrician said I should call you all." Aileen looked down at Ivy in her car seat. The baby's eyes were wide with surprise at Mrs. Merriweather's sudden arrival.

"Well, you've come to the right place!" A wide grin split Mrs. Merriweather's face in half as she grabbed Aileen's hand. As she shook it, she pulled Aileen toward her so that she could give her a half-hug with a back pat.

Alieen recoiled in the most subtle manner that she could. Grimacing, she gave the woman two tiny pats on the back and yanked herself away. Her face turned red with consternation. She'd known that she would have to get her boobs handled at this appointment, but it didn't mean she wanted any more touching than necessary.

"Come on down to the lactation station!" Mrs. Merriweather chirped. "All aboard the train to nipple town, the only place on earth where a letdown is great!"

Aileen smirked at this. This type of personality seemed to be a requirement of the job. A lactation consultant had to work with boobs all day, and with women who had various levels of comfort discussing and working with said boobs. So, of course they were over-the-top like this. The idea being that the ridiculous nature of asking a stranger about their boobs needed to be acknowledged in some way to defuse the tension.

Aileen felt too exhausted for any of this. Walking made her heartbeat thud through the flesh where her stitches were as she lugged the heavy car seat down the hall. She was losing blood constantly and still pissing pink every time she went to the bathroom. She just wanted to get this over with and get back to her house, where she could get a nap. But by the time she got the baby through this appointment, Aileen knew Ivy would be overtired and overstimulated, which would probably result in fussiness for the rest of the day.

Sleep when the baby sleeps was the biggest load of bullshit, and whoever made that phrase up deserved to be smacked in the head by a thousand sleep-deprived moms wielding diaper bags filled with enough stuff for a week-long vacation.

Her thoughts were interrupted when Mrs. Merriweather made a sudden turn down a hallway. Lining the hall were pastel pink and yellow flyers for lactation support groups, postpartum yoga, warning signs of postpartum depression, and advertisements for postpartum doulas.

"Here we are."

Mrs. Merriweather finally opened the door to an office no larger than two broom closets put together. The stale-smelling room had no windows, a flattened gray carpet, and brown water stains on the ceiling tiles. An infant scale sat in the corner, along with a sink and a small cabinet. A worn maroon couch with footstools beneath dominated the wall on the left. The walls were a sickly color that landed somewhere between orange and dark pink. Not even a hint of air flow breezed through the small, hot room.

The cramped environment pulled her back into an old memory. It was one that resurfaced and tortured her any time she had to get a pap smear or undress for a doctor. One that had made birth that much more excruciating for her, with all those people hovering about her, touching her most private areas to get to the baby, often without warning.

The memory was of an old boyfriend's bedroom with the door locked up tight. A similar feeling of foreboding came to her, the part of her that had predicted the abuse to come but had been unable to escape it back then. The image of the red jersey hanging on her boyfriend's door became stamped over her vision, permanently ingrained in her consciousness—the focal point of her dissociation during that night.

She took a deep breath and told herself that this wasn't the same; she reminded herself of where she actually was. She was here to get help from a medical professional.

"Come on in and have a seat," Mrs. Merriweather said.

Aileen might not have been able to provide an involved coparent, a big house, or any other advantages to her daughter, but breastfeeding was one thing that seemed within her ability to give, if she could just figure it out. And despite the pain and the cracked nipples—she still wanted to try.

Mrs. Merriweather's steel gray eyes were unwavering on Aileen's face while she talked. It made Aileen squirm, even though squirming made the stitches in her perineum sting even worse.

"Let's see how much milk she's getting from you, and then we can calculate how much formula you should be supplementing with."

Mrs. Merriweather took Ivy in her arms and paused on her way to the scale. "*Temporarily supplementing*, mind you!" She smiled and cooed into Ivy's face. "We don't want to get hooked on that nasty formula. No, no, no! Breast is best." She booped Ivy on the nose in a way that made Aileen clench her jaw.

Nasty formula, she'd said, as if it were drugs or something.

Aileen bit her lip when she saw the number on the scale. Still under 7 pounds, even two weeks after birth. Everything Aileen had ever heard about breastfeeding emphasized how *natural* it was. If it didn't come *naturally* to you, were you even a real woman at all? Tears welled in her eyes, but she willed them not to fall.

"Now, let's get started." Mrs. Merriweather said. "Put her to the breast, and we'll weigh her after to see how much milk is coming out."

It felt so odd to do this in a small windowless room with the door closed. Aileen would have liked someone else in the room. She would have liked for Mrs. Merriweather to leave and give her some privacy. She still hadn't gotten used to breastfeeding yet, let alone doing so in front of anyone else. Her overheated body ached for a single breeze to touch her cheek.

She gritted her teeth and lifted her shirt, determined to get it over with. Then she unlatched the front of her bra. As soon as she latched the baby to her cracked nipple, the consultant's head became an unwelcome planet in orbit around Aileen's boob.

Mrs. Merriweather watched the baby suckle and muttered to herself. Aileen's pulse thundered in her ears, and her eyes darted to the door.

Finally, Mrs. Merriweather aimed her gaze away from her breast and back at Aileen's face.

"This latch is shallow. See how her bottom lip is drawn in?" Before Aileen even had a chance to look, Mrs. Merriweather's finger was in Ivy's mouth, breaking the seal.

The newborn gave a slight squeal in protest, then stared blankly, as if she also didn't know how to respond to the sudden intrusion.

"What you're looking for," Mrs. Merriweather said as she gripped Aileen's breast, "is for her chin to touch down first, and then for the nipple to point at the roof of her mouth." With her other hand, she placed a firm hand on the baby's back and shoved her down toward the breast. With rough hands, she smashed pillows beneath Aileen's arms and jammed a rolled-up blanket under Ivy's head.

If Mrs. Merriweather had noticed Aileen flinch and stiffen at her touch, she didn't let on.

"Isn't that more comfortable?" she asked.

Aileen didn't speak. She wasn't breathing. Breastfeeding often made her feel an uncomfortable sensory overload, even when she was alone. There were so many sensations to it, most of them uncomfortable: the pinched nipples, the needle-like sting with the letdown of milk, and the ache of her neck and shoulders as she hunched over her tiny newborn. But this intervention felt like an outright assault. The image of the red jersey kept flickering into her mind's eye, making her pulse race.

Ivy latched, her bottom lip still sucked in despite the aggressive interference.

"Break the latch," Mrs. Merriweather ordered.

Aileen started to help her baby latch again, but, without warning or permission, Mrs. Merriweather palmed Ivy's head and cupped Aileen's breast, forcing the baby down onto the nipple.

"There!" Mrs. Merriweather shouted, exultant. "The perfect latch. Do you know what it was that I did differently from you?"

Aileen held back a sob. She glanced at the clock on the wall. Incredibly, only ten minutes had passed in this room. But this torture felt like it had gone on for hours.

Objectively, the latch did feel better. There wasn't a pinching sensation at her nipple. But that paled in comparison to the feeling of violation she'd just endured.

She couldn't speak, so she shook her head.

"It's quite simple, really. You just need to wait until she opens her mouth much wider!" Mrs. Merriweather put her hands on her hips and leaned back, as if she had just solved all Aileen's problems in one fell swoop.

Even though it felt like the end would never come, Aileen eventually found herself with a printed off visit summary and instructions from the consultant. She'd never been so happy to see the outdoors.

Without any meaningful ties to her parents, and with the father of her baby long gone, Aileen's only remaining support was Martha, her ex-boyfriend's mom. The breakup didn't seem to matter to Martha, who seemed hungry for someone to control, that is, *Aileen*, and her grandchild to snuggle, *Ivy*. Aileen also suspected that Martha hoped Aileen would get back together with her son and wanted to keep her in close range.

Martha was the first person to point out when Aileen gained weight or to criticize when the baby didn't have socks on during a summer day, but she was willing to babysit Ivy for free. Aileen resolved to break free of her dependence on Martha as soon as she got a better job. But for now, Aileen was still paying off the hospital bills from giving birth. As much as she loathed the woman, Martha was a necessary evil. She didn't have anybody else.

And that was the only reason she listened to Martha drone on and on during their phone call that night.

"Good for you for consulting a professional," Martha said. "I'm surprised that you were willing to admit your shortcomings like that. It's very mature of you."

Aileen bristled at the so-called *praise*. She was in her twenties, but Martha always spoke to her like she was a teenager.

Aileen sighed. "I'm starting to think that breastfeeding might be more trouble than it's worth. I'm exhausted. It hurts so bad. And pumping at work is going to be a nightmare. Sometimes I think I'd be a better mom if I just dropped this part of it and got some formula. I think Ivy deserves a more rested, patient mom. And maybe formula could give her that. That wouldn't be so bad, right?"

At this, Martha's tone soured like a bottle of 1000-day-old milk.

"Wouldn't be so bad? Are you hearing yourself? Your milk is literally your child's tether to good health. And you know what they say, Aileen. Breast is best. You said it yourself. You want what's best for Ivy. And now you want to quit when she needs you? That would be beyond selfish."

Aileen felt like she was going to throw up. It was time to change the subject. Quick.

"Listen, the reason I called is to ask for a favor."

"Oh? What's that, dear?" Martha sounded all-too pleased for an opportunity for Aileen to be even more indebted to her.

"I'm trying to find a better job and I need someone to watch Ivy for a bit so I can fill out applications. Are you available Saturday?"

Martha agreed, as she always did, and Aileen tried to ignore the revulsion she felt at being beholden to the woman, as she always did.

After the call, Ivy smiled from the pink play mat on the floor. At this age, it wasn't a real smile. It was just gas. But still, it was everything to Alieen. Aileen was too tired to smile back, though. She was always so damn tired.

She resolved to start formula.

T hat night, Aileen took Ivy to the corner store. She went to the baby aisle and eyed the rows of formula. Her pulse quickened as she looked at the dozens of options. Her head ached with indecision. Her sleep-deprived brain felt incapable of the decision. Trying to think on a scant three hours of sleep was the mental equivalent of swimming through a river of wet concrete. She wheeled the cart around the perimeter of the store, building up the courage to try again.

She roamed the liquor aisle. She could have a glass of wine that night if she used the formula instead of nursing. Just a small glass. She certainly felt like she needed it after having been manhandled by the lactation consultant earlier that day. She put a pinot grigio in the cart and turned the corner toward the baby aisle.

As she returned to the aisle with the rows of formula, she caught sight of a distinctive gray-and-pink-pinstripe pantsuit. At first, Mrs. Merriweather's face looked stunned, as if she'd been caught at something. But her features quickly smoothed over into their usual confident arrangement. She slipped a hand up and grabbed several tubes of nipple cream.

"Fancy seeing you here!" Mrs. Merriweather said. "I'm just restocking a bit. Here to grab a few groceries, are we?" Her eyes pinned Aileen to the spot and then flicked to the pinot grigio, daring her to formulate her own excuse for being in this aisle.

Aileen couldn't admit to a lactation consultant that she was here for formula, so she nodded in agreement.

"Diaper run," she explained. She grabbed a package of newborn diapers that she didn't need and placed them in the cart next to Ivy's car seat. She nodded toward the wine bottle. "And a gift for a friend's birthday."

Alieen frowned. She was an adult. Why was she lying about buying a bottle of wine? What was it about motherhood that made her feel so vulnerable to judgment?

"Don't get drawn in by the slick marketing for the formula!" Mrs. Merriweather chided, as if she could read Aileen's thoughts. "It's all lies. It's full of chemicals that will make your baby sick. Not to mention, it will reduce her IQ by multiple points."

"Oh," Aileen said, her face reddening. "Of course I wouldn't. I wasn't…"

Aileen gasped as Mrs. Merriweather came unnaturally close to her face. She could smell hazelnut coffee on her hot breath.

"If you're struggling with nursing. You can call me." She slipped a business card into Aileen's hand. Then she coiled both hands around Aileen's and squeezed.

Aileen tugged back a little, as if to release herself from the grip, but Mrs. Merriweather held fast. After a few more moments of staring intensely into Aileen's eyes until Aileen's hands ached, Mrs. Merriweather finally let go.

"I'll answer the mobile number on that card any time of day or night if you need me." She sidestepped, blocking Aileen's view of the formula. "You don't have to struggle alone."

Aileen gulped. "I'm not struggling."

Mrs. Merriweather said nothing. She just stared at Aileen, unmoving. But she smiled, standing as stiff as a statue directly in front of the formula containers. It was a standoff of sorts, and it was readily apparent that Mrs. Merriweather would not be the first one to leave this aisle.

Aileen had no other choice but to walk off empty handed.

In the morning, Aileen traveled with Ivy all the way across town to shop at a different store so she could get the formula. She forgot her phone at her apartment—there were just so many things to pack in a diaper bag with a newborn.

When Aileen returned to her apartment, there were twenty missed calls on her phone, along with several voicemails.

"Hi, Aileen. This is Mrs. Merriweather, from the lactation office. You didn't stop by the desk to make your next appointment with us, so I thought I'd call you to arrange it. Call me back soon so we can get you the help you need, okay?"

After multiple other messages saying the same exact thing, Mrs. Merriweather had left one last message saying she took the liberty of booking her for an appointment for the next day at 8:00 a.m.

Aileen tossed the phone onto the couch with disgust.

"Like I'm going to go there again."

The phone buzzed with another call. And another. Ivy, impatient in her car seat, started to mewl. Aileen stared the phone down. Her hands turned into fists. She stalked over and picked it up.

"What?" she shouted.

"I just wanted to confirm your appointment for tomorrow at 8:00 a.m."

Aileen chewed on her bottom lip before answering. "I can't make it tomorrow. I'm sorry."

"Well how about next week?"

"I don't need any more appointments. We're good."

"You're good?" Mrs. Merriweather let a hint of disbelief enter her voice. "After I just saw you in the formula aisle yesterday? You're good? Is that what Ivy's pediatrician said?"

"No. I..." Aileen felt dizzy. She hated confrontation, but she had to tell the truth to get this woman off her back. "I decided to do formula. So, I won't be needing any more appointments."

"Oh," Mrs. Merriweather said, her voice maudlin. "Oh no."

"Okay. Well, have a nice day," Aileen said.

"Wait! Let's think this over. It's so early to call it quits. Tell me what the problem is, and we'll think of a solution together."

Aileen's voice trembled. "I'm feeling really uncomfortable. You need to stop this and stop calling me."

"But your daughter is depending on you. Are you really going to give up? If you do this, you'll—"

Aileen hung up the phone. She hugged herself for several moments to stop her arms from shaking. Once the tremors stopped, she picked Ivy up out of the car seat and swayed, letting herself be calmed by the steady rhythm of her daughter's breathing and the scent of her milky breath. She traced the delicate, downy swirl of hair at the crown of Ivy's head and ran her fingers over the dimples on Ivy's plump hands. Aileen's troubles were diluted by Ivy's sweetness, and her heartbeat slowed as Ivy reached a hand up to stroke her cheek.

All else shrunk in importance. Ivy was all that mattered, and she was safe, *safe*, in Aileen's arms. Ivy fell asleep in time, and Aileen followed her down into a deep slumber.

I vy seemed brand new after having the formula. Her usual squalling had been replaced by gentle wiggles and yawns. And for the first time ever, Ivy slept more than an hour at once, and so did Aileen.

The only downside was explaining the switch to Martha when she called to arrange the last-minute details for dropping Ivy off Saturday. Martha said the typical propaganda from the *breast is best* camp, but Alieen felt immune to it. Nothing was more convincing to her than the serene expression on her daughter's face and the end to her baby's constant discomfort.

Before Aileen went to bed that night, she opened her phone to a barrage of emails and text messages from Mrs. Merriweather.

The last message made the hairs on Aileen's arms stand up.

You'll regret this. Call me back. K??

Aileen blocked Mrs. Merriweather's email and phone number.

I n the morning, Aileen drove to Martha's house and dropped Ivy off with four full bottles of formula, feeling smug about the fact that she'd only had to pump for her comfort and not with the anxiety of hoping she'd make enough milk to last the day.

She returned to her apartment and changed into comfortable pajamas, allowing herself an hour to nap undisturbed. By the afternoon, she was hours deep into her job search, feeling rejuvenated and empowered. Maybe she could rock this motherhood thing after all. She had just clicked a job listing and started to upload her resume when the doorbell rang.

At first, she ignored it. She had so little time to herself, and she wasn't going to waste it on a solicitor.

When the doorbell continued to ring for several minutes, Aileen got up and strode to the door.

Mrs. Merriweather stood on her welcome mat.

"What the fuck?" Aileen exclaimed.

"You wouldn't answer my calls."

"I don't need your services anymore. The baby isn't even here right now, so you can just go back to your office and manhandle somebody else's boobs. I'm done."

Mrs. Merriweather seemed to look around for something, and seeming satisfied, she stepped forward, crossing the threshold. Aileen would realize later that Mrs. Merriweather had been looking for witnesses.

"I told you that you'd regret this. It didn't have to be this way."

"I'm calling the police. You can't be here. You need to leave me and my—"

Mrs. Merriweather gave Aileen a hard shove that knocked her off balance.

"Ow!" Aileen landed hard on the floor.

Mrs. Merriweather moved fast. Before Aileen could stand back up, Mrs. Merriweather had grabbed an eight-ounce glass baby bottle from the counter. She reared it back and struck Aileen in the head.

Aileen's vision went dark.

———

Aileen awoke with zip ties binding her wrists. Her eyes adjusted to the sight of stone bricks and iron bars around her. A small, stained cot and a filthy toilet occupied the corners of the room. The air was cold and subterranean, her breath forming clouds as it left her mouth. It smelled like shit, piss, mold, and something sour she couldn't quite place.

Beyond her cell she saw other rooms identical to her own, all lit by heavy metal sconces with eerie green flames that seemed to pulse like a heartbeat.

The sound of Mrs. Merriweather's voice was a distant murmur in Aileen's ears. It was difficult to maintain consciousness. Her head ached where she'd been bludgeoned, and she gritted her teeth. She had to stay conscious. She had to stay sharp.

Aileen wasn't wearing a shirt, and she watched, frozen with horror, as Mrs. Merriweather placed each of Aileen's breasts in a plastic breast shield. The sight of crusted blood on the rims of the shields shocked Aileen into action. Alieen tried to bat the breast pump away with her numb hands, but her reactions felt slow, like she'd been drugged.

Mrs. Merriweather hummed as she worked, unfazed by Aileen's pathetic attempt at struggle. She attached the shields to the breast pump and wound the whole apparatus with duct tape, affixing it tight to her skin. Without warning, she turned on the machine and swung the dial to the highest suction setting.

Aileen screamed.

"You just wouldn't listen, would you?"

Aileen yelped and howled with pain. Somehow this device seemed stronger than any pump she had tried on her own. Her nipples scraped the sides of the flanges, which seemed two sizes too small. The first liquid to drip down into the containers wasn't milk—it was blood from Aileen's contorted, cracked nipples.

Mrs. Merriweather watched with flat, gray eyes. "If we don't feed them, everything gets much worse, believe me."

Aileen fought to speak through the pain, desperate to understand what was happening.

"Feed *who*?"

"Don't shoot the messenger," Mrs. Merriweather continued in a chirpy voice. "I'm not the one who controls this." She stroked Aileen's damp, sweaty hair in a twisted, maternal fashion.

Aileen parted her sandpaper lips and panted through the most painful letdown of milk she'd ever experienced. It felt like razors were being shoved through her breast tissue. The milk came out pink, since it was mixed with her blood.

"I need water," she gasped.

Mrs. Merriweather said nothing. She looked at her watch, seeming to have better things to do.

"I need water for the milk!" Aileen insisted. "I haven't had anything to drink for a long time."

"Oh, silly me!" Mrs. Merriweather stood and nodded, seeming to approve of this reasoning. "You can't make milk if you aren't drinking water. I'll be right back."

As soon as Mrs. Merriweather was gone, Aileen crawled toward the front of her cell. The pump and its parts dragged painfully across the rough stones, pulling on her already distorted and twisted breasts. She peered across the hall into another cell. Another woman was there, and she was also strapped to a breast pump. Even in the dim light, Aileen could see that the woman looked frail and wasted, as if she never moved from the cot.

"Hey!" Aileen called out. "Over here!"

The woman barely turned her head at the sound. Her eyes glinted darkly in the light. Then she closed them and turned her back to Aileen.

Aileen turned her head. The hall held dozens of other rooms. Dozens of other mothers. And yet, the only sounds were soft groans and the shushing of vacuum suction.

"Who are we feeding? Why are you doing this?" Aileen demanded when Mrs. Merriweather returned.

Mrs. Merriweather sighed, as if she were put out by Aileen's question.

"In my experience, it will just upset you more to know anything. After the rigors of childbirth, you'd think you lot would have stronger stomachs, but it is what it is."

"I don't care. I want to know. I can handle it."

Aileen's pleading was ignored.

"This is all you need to know: If you are a good producer and don't try to escape, we'll move you to one of the nicer rooms. We may even let you go one day. Good behavior will get you far. *Begging* will get you nowhere."

Aileen gritted her teeth. She'd seen the woman across from her. None of them were being let go. Not ever.

"I want to know whose children I'm feeding instead of my own," Aileen said.

"You won't like it." Mrs. Merriweather tsked, turning toward the exit.

"Let me feed them directly instead of with this pump," Aileen blurted in desperation.

Eyebrows raised, Mrs. Merriweather turned back toward her. "Nobody's ever asked that before. But still, I'm afraid that's not possible."

"You're a lactation consultant, right? You know that a baby is more effective at pulling milk than even the best pump. Let me feed the baby directly, and I'll be a better producer. Why would you do things this way, with pumps?" Aileen hoped there *were* infants somewhere to feed. It was a desperate guess.

Mrs. Merriweather pursed her lips. "We use the pumps, because you wouldn't be able to handle feeding this kind of child."

"Try me."

Mrs. Merriweather shook her head, looking irritated.

"I want to get out of here and earn my freedom. I'll do the best job I can." She looked down at the machine strapped to her chest. "And I hate pumping. Won't you give me a chance? It will be better for my supply. I haven't breastfed for over twenty-four hours. Look at this pathetic output. What I *need* is a baby. Otherwise, you'll get nothing from me."

Mrs. Merriweather frowned at the empty bottles protruding from Aileen's breasts. There were a few drops of milk, but mostly a scant misting of blood.

"Fine," Mrs. Merriweather said with a strange smile. "But don't say I didn't warn you."

She ripped the strips of duct tape off Aileen's chest. A layer of skin ripped off with it, and Aileen's eyes watered from the stinging, burning pain. Still, the breast shields fell to the ground, and it was a slight relief. Mrs. Merriweather turned off the pump. Mrs. Merriweather left, leaving the pump with Aileen.

A few minutes later, Mrs. Merriweather returned with a squirming, burlap bundle in her arms. The baby's entire body and face were covered. With her arms too full to manage much else, she left the cell door cracked behind her.

"You see, my master is the reason for all of this. I serve him by caring for his children. He's only a lesser demon, so his children can't walk in our world. He doesn't have the power to tether them. Thankfully, there's another way."

She leaned over so that Aileen could see, and she pulled down the burlap.

The *child*, if it could be called this, in Mrs. Merriweather's arms was slimy, dark green, and covered in pustules. Its eyes glowed a dark yellow and were threaded with bulging red veins.

Aileen muffled a scream by biting into her hand. She tasted copper.

"After they're born, there's a short window of time, during which the spawn can be on earth. If they're fed human milk during that time, they can stay here. If they don't get it regularly for the first year, they get sick and fade away. My master has an interest in amassing an army of them, and I'm more than happy to oblige."

Mrs. Merriweather tickled the cheek of the snarling demon. When it opened its mouth, two rows of sharp, needle-like teeth sprung out from its blackened gums.

"I'd do it myself, but I can't lactate. Even if I could, there are too many of them for one woman to feed alone. My master allows me to serve in this way. I bring him the nursemaids. The mothers of spawn don't typically survive birth. You know what they say, don't you?"

"What?" Aileen asked. She felt numb as she watched the squirming demon spawn stretch its misshapen arms toward her.

"It takes a village! That's what they say!"

Mrs. Merriweather leaned over, thrusting the clawing creature into Aileen's chest. The infant's breath smelled like decay and brimstone as it opened its hungry mouth, aiming toward Aileen's nipple to latch on. A viscous glob of rancid phlegm slipped off its bulbous purple tongue and onto Aileen's chest. She gagged.

The hungry mouth closed over her breast with needle teeth, and fireworks of pain appeared in Aileen's vision. Aileen yanked on the demon, but it held on like a lion to its prey. She pulled harder, as every signal from her body screamed that something was very, very wrong. Finally, she succeeded, and tore it from her, throwing the little demon. It landed on the cot.

Shock made Alieen feel nothing when she noticed that the demon still had a large hunk of her flesh in its jaws. It chewed on the bleeding piece of her, seeming to relish its prize. It had taken most of her breast with it when she'd ripped it away. As it chewed, it teetered on the edge of the cot, nearly about to hit its head on the hard stone floor.

Mrs. Merriweather shrieked and dove to rescue the creature. With Mrs. Merriweather's back turned, Aileen grabbed the cube-shaped pump and slammed it into Mrs. Merriweather's head. Mrs. Merriweather hit the floor as the demon squalled and rolled onto the ground. Mrs. Merriweather growled and pushed herself up, but Aileen was there with the tubing connected to the pump. She wrapped the plastic tubing around Mrs. Merriweather's neck and squeezed until the woman's feet stopped kicking. She let the body drop to the floor and burst through the cracked door. She closed and locked it with a deftness that surprised herself.

Mrs. Merriweather came to and shrieked with rage.

Aileen ran down the hall, ascended the steps, and fumbled her way to the door. Blood streamed from her chest where the demon had taken its bite. She heard the cries of Mrs. Merriweather not far behind. She burst through the door and down a series of office hallways until she found herself back in the lactation office waiting room.

Blinking in the bright lights after coming out of the dank dungeon, she whipped her head around, shouting warnings at the other young mothers.

She wasn't wearing a top, and her chest bled and oozed. She dashed out the front door. Blinded by tears and pain, she didn't stop running until a police officer grabbed her from the side of the road.

Later, when she awoke in the hospital, she was told that they couldn't save one breast, but that she shouldn't worry, because she could still breastfeed with just one. Aileen was too tired to tell them that she wanted to do formula. In her haze of pain, she saw Martha bring Ivy to her one remaining breast to feed. Aileen was too weak to protest.

By the time Aileen convinced police officers to check out the alleged dungeon in the office basement, it was several days after her escape. She walked them down the corridor of the lactation office and down the long hallway until they reached the end. The door that had led down to the dungeon was gone.

Neither was there any record of anyone named Mrs. Merriweather who had ever worked there. The officers looked on her with pity in their eyes as they refused her request to demolish the drywall, even after Aileen pointed out patches of wet paint. They sent her to a doctor instead.

After that, the diagnosis was swift and definitive—postpartum psychosis. Aileen took the medicines as prescribed. And they did make her feel better. She began to accept the fact that she'd made up the entire lactation encounter because of stress and sleep deprivation.

Weeks passed, and Aileen started to heal from her wounds. Then one early morning, at a coffee shop with Ivy's car seat on her arm, Aileen's attention drifted to a business flyer taped to the bulletin board. The pink paper with gray trim stood out from the others, and it listed the address of a new business downtown.

A business by the name of *Mrs. Merriweather's Lactation Services*.

She snatched it with trembling hands, ripped it into shreds, and threw it into the trash can, drawing a curious look from the barista.

Under her door, a few weeks after Ivy fell ill, there came a letter written on pink stationery.

· · ·

Dearest Aileen,

My associate, Martha, whom you may know, has told me some vital information. Previously, I was unaware that the timid girl who walked into my clinic was the surviving mother of a spawn.

We shall not pursue you further, since you harbor a child of our master. Continue to raise the child as you see fit but remember—if you want your daughter to remain on this earth, breast is best. It takes one year to tether them.

You might not believe me, since she doesn't look like the spawn you saw in our center. But I assure you, she is. The others look like monsters because they didn't get milk from the beginning like your little darling.

Is she fading yet? She needs human milk. Fast.

Sincerely,
Your Lactation Specialist

An address was written at the bottom of the letter. Aileen took the pink paper and crumpled it in her fist. She couldn't lactate anymore. Not after so many weeks without having done it. And Ivy needed milk *now*. She *had* started fading. *Failure to thrive*, the pediatrician had said, and they'd yet to find a cause even after weeks of testing.

Those women were still held prisoner there at the lactation office, no doubt. Aileen didn't need much from them—just a little until she could start lactating again. She couldn't let Ivy fade away.

Ivy was all that mattered.

Mrs. Merriweather would help in the name of one of the spawn, surely.

Aileen dialed Martha's number.

"Can you watch Ivy for me today? I need to go back to the lactation office. It's an emergency."

"Of course, dear. I never stopped watching her. I'll *never* stop watching her."

Aileen clenched her jaw, hating Martha more in that moment than she ever had. If her ex had been a literal demon, what did that make his mother?

"Why didn't you tell me?" Aileen asked. "If you knew what was going on at Mrs. Merriweather's, why didn't you warn me about what I'd find? Why didn't you warn *her* I was coming? Why didn't you tell me who your *goddamned son* was?"

She might still have both breasts if Martha hadn't kept everything from her.

Martha let out a heavy sigh. "Would you have believed me?"

Aileen said nothing. She wouldn't have.

"There are some things you have to see with your own eyes to understand."

"Would you have left Ivy motherless? Left me to rot in there?"

"I would have come to get you. Eventually. I can't be running after you every day. I had other mothers to attend to. My son is rather busy, so I've been rather busy. And it wasn't my fault you decided to rip your breast off rather than go along with the program. You really should work on taking responsibility for your actions. Everyone's always to blame but Aileen."

The back of Aileen's throat burned, and her finger yearned to end the call. But Ivy coughed, sounding pitiful and weak, and still sweeter than she had any right to be. It tore Aileen's heart to shreds beneath her one remaining breast.

It takes a village.

Ivy was all that mattered.

"I'm going back. To get Ivy some milk. She's getting weak."

"And you want to, even though you've seen what they do there? Even though you experienced it firsthand?" Martha sounded amused.

Ivy was all that mattered.

There may have been demons in her world, but Aileen would have been willing to become any worse kind of evil for the chance to save her daughter.

"Just come. Come as soon as you can."

A RISE IN RED

SUMIKO SAULSON

E bony stares down
As the tiniest whirlpool
Spirals crimson through the water
The roar of her flush
As she depresses the toilet handle
The bleeding is ceaseless
She can't stop the flow
She begins to feel dizzy
And crashes to the floor
She hears blaring through the bathroom walls
The bombastic fantastic baritone
Of the televangelist blasting
Through the speakers of her grandmother's

Ancient cathode ray television set

Revelation and End-Times

And Ebony pregnant

She lives in the wrong State:

Of poverty, of being, and

Above all, the Union

Grandmother changes who she is channeling

Crystal gazes Forty-Seven's numerology

No horns rise upon his crown

Of televised thorns to tell Grandmother,
The man in charge has risen up from hell

His red right hand a rich con man

A thirteenth spawn denied

How many blood sacrifices

Will this Devil require?

Airplanes falling from the skies

Revelation 6:13

Terror trickles down in this economy

Skips past a back-alley abortion

Dark shadows loom over poverty

Black women die in childbirth

At four times the frequency

For Ebony, this is no vague possibility nor theoretical fatality

A rise in red from waters churning below

As she bleeds out her wounded womb

No preacher man is present to prevent

This miscarriage of justice

EXCEPTIONAL WRETCHES

JOE KOCH

"The American dream is pure pornography," says Glen. He's been snorting amethyst all morning, so it's hard to keep up with him. I don't mind struggling and getting out of breath for this. If things work out, his connection is going to save my life.

Sure, I trust him. Why wouldn't I? We've been partners since the last unemployment purge. We're staying off the lists, living under the radar, making it work.

Glen fidgets at a crosswalk, waiting for the interminable traffic to stop. He taps his foot, peering left and right. "See, like what the fuck do you mean by the dream, dreaming on stolen land? Whose dream are they talking about? Not the people who lived here first, got murdered or infected with our germs, kids put in camps. Not the people imported like merch and sold to white land owners, still getting sold for prison labor. It's always been the same lie, the same gloss of nonreality. You've got to learn to see through the packaging."

"Yeah," I gasp. "We're lucky we're white."

"That's just more packaging. You got to learn to look deep."

The walking man icon blinks from across the street. This particular crosswalk light upsets me because the walking man has no circle for a head, just a jagged stick-man rushing to nowhere in a headless hurry. The sight makes my stomach lurch.

Glen launches off the curb, leaving me behind. I'm taking two steps to his one, or maybe one and a half, to keep up with his longer stride, gasping for breath in the fog of exhaust. My condition has gotten worse in the past few months.

I'll be better soon. We're on our way to get the juice.

Cars honk and nudge forward even though we have the right of way according to the signs. Ever since some AI program confused "pedophile" with "pedestrian" drivers have been getting more and more aggressive. They're talking about making it illegal to walk anywhere soon, and cars these days are the size of tanks. Having a big guy like Glen at my side has probably saved my life more than a few times.

Once we land on the opposite curb unscratched, we're heading under the highway bridges where the echoes of traffic are less deafening, the airborne toxins less redolent. I say, "The packaging. Getting past it. That's what the juice is for, right?"

Glen stops dead and I trip over my own feet, landing in the garbage and weeds. At least the ground is soft here.

He glares down at me. "Look here, little man, the juice isn't for everybody."

I pick myself up so I don't look like I'm groveling. I've done enough groveling just to get Glen to take me this far. "Well, if you don't mind my pointing it out, that sounds pretty elitist to me. Don't you think? Doesn't everyone deserve equal access?"

"That's what I mean by the lie. Inalienable rights never applied to anyone but the elite. The men who wrote that shit kept slaves, for Christ's sake."

"Oh, honey, don't be like this." I tilt my head and eyeball his groin and chest. I'm not above a little bit of emotional manipulation if it gets the job done. Or in this case, if it gets me the juice. "We've been over this already. We both know it's not the right time. Let's get this done before it's too late to take care of it."

Glen remains stern in visage. I'm not too worried. I know him well enough to recognize his silence as a preamble to agreement. But then he surprises me.

"I hope you'll forgive me."

He pulls me into his arms, kisses the top of my head, and places a hand on my abdomen. My stomach somersaults, not only because of my condition, the exhaust, and stress, but because of what Glen says next.

"It's not too late to go back to how things were, little man."

I'd like to shove him away, but I have to be soft about it. For all his wild ideas, Glen has never been able to understand the simple fact that it's not a matter of choice for me. Finding a cure is essential to my survival. This is a matter of life and death.

"Can you trust me?" I say. Gently, gently. "Can't you at least try? Trust me as much as I trust you. We made a plan. We're partners. Let's get on with it, okay?"

He nods downward with uncharacteristic gravity, and sniffs hard. Peering left and right, he pulls out the baggie of the purple stuff and takes a quick hit, licking his finger before a loud, deep snort and then rubbing his gums with the residue. When he looks up at me again, his eyes are vibrant and clear.

"Fair enough, little man. Let's rock."

Dang, I'd sure like some of that clarity. What I wouldn't give for the relief of being high and able to breathe easily again, even if it's just for a few minutes. But I have to abstain. I need to be clean so the juice can do its work. I haven't eaten or taken so much as a sip for three whole days.

We're through the weeds and beyond the shadows of concrete pillars below the overpass now, into the dense, empty heart of the city. Towering skyscrapers are encircled by tiers of twisting highways like the ones knotted and screaming with traffic over our heads. Tires wail across concrete like creatures in endless agony. Raw nerve endings of exit ramps are blockaded, sealing off this forbidden sector, a city within the city, a city like an aneurism, a downtown that might have once thrived but is now the squatting place of undesirables, the disappeared, the legally dead. Anyone who isn't wanted elsewhere winds up here if they're too weak or too wily to go to rehabilitation camp, anyone with something to hide.

You'd think it was deserted at first glance. From this vantage point on the perimeter, the streets and sidewalks are populated only by trash. Plastics, defunct machinery, car parts, shattered glass. The city within the city, a stomach unable to digest its rotting past.

Move closer as we do, and in between the looming skyscrapers with hundreds of stacked, vacant eyes, you'll find small, ancient structures. Centuries-old houses sandwiched beside churches and graveyards; fences around mounds of decayed nothing, and tiny kiosks whose former purpose is impossible to know. Forgotten currencies fade on crumbling price signs. Everywhere, peeling paint and broken windows, and at this point you'd think you better get out of there, and I'd have said exactly that to Glen if this wasn't urgent. If the thing growing inside me wasn't making me into someone else, someone I don't recognize.

Glen slows as we go deeper. His voice gets quieter, but it doesn't stop. He's a man with a lot of opinions.

"Freedom isn't free, little man. It's the most expensive commodity going, costs millions of lives. No just people, either. Look around. You see any wildlife except rats and pigeons? Cockroaches? Any tree that ain't collapsed or diseased? It's more addictive than amethyst. Once you get a taste of freedom—see, this is what I'm trying to tell you. You'll always want more. It's never enough."

I should keep my mouth shut, but Glen is really getting on my nerves. "You're being awfully presumptuous. That's CEO talk and you know I'm not like that. All I want is a fair chance at life."

"I'm just saying that when some people see the real truth about themselves, about everything, they can't handle it. You might not like what you see."

"The real truth about my damn self is the one thing I know inimitably well so you can just stop with your—"

"Okay, okay, keep your voice down." Glen's hand presses my shoulder in a misguided effort at calming me. The weight adds to my physical burden and throws me off balance. I stumble against a lamppost.

Glen glances around from left to right as I wheeze and cling to the cool metal. I stare down at the colorful disgorged wires at the broken base, trying to focus on something besides my body.

He says, "I hope you won't judge me. That you'll remember us the way we were."

The thing inside me saps my strength and sickens me, spinning on an axis like a fatty, fleshy planet churning my viscera from within and making me dizzy. It isn't happy that I've starved it. I feel it bloating against my bladder and lower ribs as if straining to get out. I whisper, "Soon enough, you little shit."

Glen says, "The fuck did you say?"

"I said I need to take a piss."

"Better wait until I find the temple and we get inside."

"This isn't optional."

"It's not far, if I've tracked it right. You can make it. You'll be fine."

The tension of the thing inside fighting me is a live wire tightening between my urethra and chest, scorching me from heart to groin. I lurch toward an alley with my knees clamped together and scoot behind a dumpster. The pain lingers after relieving myself, but at least now I can stand up straight again.

Without Glen's yammering, I notice as I dry off that this far into the city, the sound of the highways has faded to distant white noise. The quiet in the absence of cars stuns me.

People chatter from afar in voices that lack hostility. I hear laughter, maybe children, although that hardly seems possible since the media says this forgotten slum is a place of violence and neglect where the disenfranchised go to die. I wonder if that's true. We've seen a few elderly shuffling by cloaked in blankets, but much less trash amassed than on the outskirts, and no sign of the tent encampments full of disease-ridden indigents I was led to expect. Even in this dark alley, no predators lurk, no used needles litter the cracked thoroughfare. Sunlight unfiltered by smog reflects in cheerful sparkles from the puddle of urine at my feet.

I'm almost ashamed to have befouled the place.

"Here it is," says Glen as I emerge from the alley. "What did I tell you? We were right here all the time and you had to piss in the street."

He shakes his head at me and nods toward a building with a silly, overwrought classical façade. Skyscrapers crowd its shoulders like thugs. Long ago it must have been the tallest structure in the city aside from the church steeple. Five stories of ornate molded concrete stand surprisingly intact, capering with baroque figures, theatrical faces, and mythical beasts.

Where any reasonable architect would have carved one gargoyle, it sports three. For each unfurling frond of imaginary vegetation, there swarms a plethora of beetles, mice, feathered creatures, and bees. In bold relief above the massive double doors, waves of copulating men, satyrs, and livestock spell out the structure's name in a playful, perverse font: Brotherhood of the Shining Bull, est. 1893.

Inside is gold and parquet, a theater of sorts. No one attends or guards as we walk through the front doors, which are not barricaded or locked. Not what I'd expect in such a supposedly dangerous spot.

Glen's hand on my shoulder again. This time I'm prepared to resist the disorienting weight. "Last chance to turn back, little man. Are you sure you want to go through with this? It's your choice."

Incredulous, I say, "Do you want me dead?"

"Hey, don't be dramatic. We can make things work. Just say the word. You know I got your back."

"If you don't want to be here, this is a fine time to leave. I can find my way back."

"No way, I would never do that to you."

"Really, feel free. I'm all set."

"Little man, why you want to hurt me like that? That's cold. I don't want you to regret—"

"Welcome, fellow riders of the Great Bull," says a man, loud enough to kindly interrupt our argument. He strides into the lobby as if he's expecting us. As if we're old buddies. Maybe he's like this with everyone.

He's buff as hell and bigger than Glen. Unlike Glen, he's dressed like a character in one of those old gladiator movies, wearing a short, white, belted toga-like thing that would read as a dress if he wasn't two-hundred and seventy-five pounds of hard muscle. He looks ridiculous, but somehow, you can't laugh at him. He brims over with good-humored ease and unassailable self-assurance. Not one quiver of anxiety ripples below his skin, no specter of gender confusion or discomfort with sexual preferences haunts his calm, smiling eyes.

I blurt out, probably too loudly, "I want the juice!"

Glen balks. "Whoa, play it cool, little man, not so fast."

"Certainly," says the gladiator dude. "Right this way."

He makes to stroll back into the larger amphitheater area he came from, motions for us to follow. Glen's arm shoots out across me as I rush forward. I almost cold cock my throat on it.

"Just a minute there, friend," he says to the gladiator dude. "We negotiate first."

"Negotiate?"

"Yeah, you know, like the full terms."

"There are no terms. All are welcome to partake."

"Sure, you say that now, then you up the price later. We're not falling for that old game."

"Glen, cut it out."

"Hey, little man, I'm here to look out for you, okay? You were about to walk into the deal totally blind. So how about it, pal." He turns to the gladiator dude again. "Give us the full low-down or we're out of here."

"Glen, no! That's not, we're not—he doesn't speak for me. I don't care what it costs. Please, just ignore him."

The gladiator dude tilts his head and looks at Glen, puzzled. "I'm sorry, why exactly are you here?"

"I'm an ally. I'm here to make sure people like you don't go around taking advantage of the vulnerable and marginalized."

"Jesus Christ." I clench my brow in agony. This whole thing is giving me a headache. Sometimes Glen makes me feel like I'm going insane.

"Unfortunately," the gladiator dude says, "I can't name a price for you. I'm very sorry not to accommodate."

No no no no no no.

I'm ready to get on my knees and beg. Fuck self-respect.

"Oh yeah?" says Glen, trying to look as big as the gladiator dude and not quite measuring up. "Why's that? What kind of scam are you guys trying to pull here?"

Gladiator dude shrugs.

I collapse and start dumping out my backpack. Jewelry, watches, water credits, medications, food vouchers, ID cards. "These numbers are good," I tell him. "Five of these alone. The people are dead but they haven't been registered. No criminal history. You can cross any border, go anywhere. This diamond ring, I've got the papers for it right here, see? You can have it all, everything I've got. Please."

Crouching, he takes the backpack away from me and puts each item inside after a brief examination. I can't read his expression to tell if this is a good sign or not, but I'm giddy with hope. Glen stands over us, more jittery than ever, bopping from one foot to the other like he's doing a little dance.

We stand up together. Holding the backpack, gladiator dude says, "That's quite a haul. You must have scavenged and gone without, suffered for a long time to come up with all of that."

"Gotcha!" Glen yelps as if he's ready to celebrate.

Gladiator dude ignores him and hands me the backpack. "Keep it. Your suffering is over. Our sacrament is free. All who wish to ride the Great Bull will take their seat upon his back."

"That's amazing, but really, but I'll pay you. I don't mind."

"No. We refuse all material donations. We're fully capable of meeting our own needs with the self-contained and renewable resources we have here. Payment is not necessary. Furthermore, we require no ablutions or labor in exchange for what we offer. It is a precious resource, and our gift. Soon it will be yours, too. This way."

I follow like an excited puppy. Glen mutters to me, "I don't trust this clown. There has to be a catch."

It occurs to me—and the thought is a little disturbing—that despite all Glen's lecturing about the juice, he's never had it. He couldn't have. He's never been here before. Maybe he got it second hand, and somebody ripped him off, made him pay for it; but if the juice does everything he says it does, how would he not see through the lie after having it? More importantly, why would he lie to me and pretend he's partaken?

I'll ask him later. Right now I can't let anything come between me and the juice.

The thing inside me is squirming, if a planet can be said to squirm. I picture it sometimes as a teeming membrane, like a water balloon full of worms; as a gaseous globe condensing into stagnant liquid discharge that makes me retch; or as a monstrous blinking thing made of congealed light, eyes, and wings, primed to explode.

A bomb made of meat, with a will of its own, and all it wants to do is eat me and keep eating until there's nothing of me left. They say every man and every woman is a star but this thing feels more like a black hole.

We follow the gladiator dude through the amphitheater area. The only seats are in the balconies and opera boxes above. The floor is dedicated to different gym equipment, sparring rings, and wrestling mat set ups. Men of different heights and shapes and skin tones—but all as buff as hell—are working out, stretching, climbing, lifting, fighting, and fucking right out in the open. Clothes appear to be highly optional. If the men wear anything, it's the same toga-like thing as our friendly guide.

As we head up to the stage, we pass an intense, quiet threesome with several enrapt spectators. They nod to us, unperturbed as they stroke themselves, and then go back to watching the three men in the center who moan and breathe, deep and slow, as if fucking this way were some sort of meditation practice. Glen twitches and mutters in my ear, "Disgusting."

"Dude, can you not?"

"I mean, not out in public like this."

"I think it's kind of hot."

"Don't get in over your head, little man. We take what we need and get the hell out of here. I'm not signing up for any cult."

I don't tell Glen, but I'm beginning to wonder if signing up would really be so bad. No one here seems stressed out or starving. There's no cameras or cops. And going up the stairs behind the gladiator dude gives me a great view of his ass.

Up on the stage, a large urn connected to tubes and chemistry set-type shit is set up on an altar. It's warm up here. It smells great. The fragrance in the entire space is pleasant, nothing like a locker room or gym or seedy club like you'd expect. The gladiator dude presents me with a small wooden bowl that he takes from a stack on the altar. With a long ladle, also made of some kind of rustic carved wood, he dips into the urn, stirs, and then serves me about a shot glass-sized quantity of the warm pearlescent liquid.

The juice.

"That's all it takes?" I ask.

"It's quite potent," says the gladiator dude. "That's enough for both of you."

As I raise the bowl to my lips, Glen takes hold of my arm, almost spilling the elixir that will fix me forever and save my life.

"Potent, huh?" His eyes dart around. He hunches away from the gladiator dude and whispers to me. "What if it's, you know, bull juice. Like for real. Don't you want to know what's in this?"

"No. Let go of me."

"You don't care what you're putting into your body?"

"No."

Still restraining my arm, Glen's face twists. He looks awful and sweaty, especially compared to the men here. His breath is full of the chemical tang of amethyst. He pleads, "What about the baby?"

I say, "Fuck the baby."

He slams the bowl out of my hands. He kicks it away across the stage. I'm gasping, left shaking at the sudden violence from him, not quite registering it. He's never done anything like this.

No longer pleading, still sweaty, and looking very pleased with himself, Glen stands back and smiles. A noise builds from outside, a thump, thump, thump of displaced air. Like a helicopter.

Glen yells, "You're under arrest."

I hear a warbled voice giving orders from a megaphone outside. I can't tell what they're saying. There's no time to process any of this.

I kick Glen in the shins. He yells. I kick again. He grabs for my leg, his head down. I slam his skull with my backpack. He reels. He's at the edge of the stage. I shove as hard as I can.

He tumbles over the edge, hits the floor hard. I swing around and grab the urn from the altar. I gulp down the contents, chugging the juice like I'm shot-gunning a beer.

It's warm through my core, dribbling down my face, soaking my shirt.

When I'll choke if I swallow another drop, I toss it and take off running.

I'm past storage rooms and hallways, through an industrial-sized kitchen and out the back by an emergency exit in under a minute. Not only is the outdoors behind the temple mercifully cop-free, it also looks like I landed on another planet. Some sort of park, as big as a forest, as far as I can see. I dart between the trees. They're so tall that it's like the sun has set in the dense patches. I'm running, no sign of helicopter or megaphone. I hear only my breath, twigs snapping under my feet, the whisper of unsettled leaves.

I keep running with no idea where I'll wind up. The forest never seems to end. The juice has dried on my face and shirt. Sloppy and thirsty, I stop near a brook and listen for footsteps, gunshots, hollering. Nothing but gently trickling brook.

The water sparkles where the sun sneaks through the high canopy. I can't remember if there's danger in drinking water that's not bottled. Seems like I've been warned about it, everything should be sealed in plastic, it's the American way. But what if they lied, and who cares now? I'm destined for a breeding camp until I've exhausted my fertility if they catch me. I'll no longer be me, just a body farmed for its resources, a spiritual dustbowl where everything native is ripped out and replaced to grow something never meant to be.

I'm splashing water on my face and slurping handfuls on my knees when it hits me. The baby is out.

The baby is all around me.

This planet, this forest, this stream. The bomb is going off. The flesh is learning to weave. The black hole is permeated by starry light, and it has finally begun relinquishing its terrible gravity.

All things move toward freedom. The juice is working. The particles are reassembling. They could be cult members, speeding cars, ancient trees in a circular glade. All chaos is not just possible but probable. In its most extreme manifestation, life is entropy. The little planet that grew and spun and gnawed has sickened me because for too long I kept it inside. For too long I let it go hungry.

We're one and yet not the same. Before the invasion, this land lay swathed in dense forest. Cutting down the old growth kills me. I'm no one. I don't belong here. I'm everyone. I'm made of plastic. I'm a dead continent covered in weakened monoculture. Amber waves of grain and corn rot in me, ghostless with the absence of many extinct species. I'm drunk with denial, buried by memories of genocide.

The baby is hungry.

I'm up and running again, clamoring through pre-history, through the forest dark and verdant, turning over rocks and branches, splashing through streams; looking inside my cruel baby and metamorphosing into the wrong dream. The juice is in me. We are one and yet not the same. We call for wolves, and wolves metastasize. My baby grows like a disease. I'm larger, stronger, faster, bursting through my clothes, swelling with insatiable greed.

I'm all muscle and blood, the beating heart of the invader, and Glen was right about one thing. I don't like what I see.

I'm the beating heart of the invader, beating the ground into submission with my pounding feet, tearing the wind to shreds with my hungry teeth, and slashing my way across the blood meridian toward another new frontier, and then another, manifesting my destiny without end, because I will always be in my infancy.

I take everything. I am everywhere. I can tear you apart and eat you alive, and I will not apologize. This land is my land. This baby is my property.

I crash through the emergency exit and back inside the temple, raving. I don't know how I got here. My clothes are gone, shredded by my grotesquely exaggerated physicality. I race naked through the kitchen and down the halls, growing larger, faster, bursting into the amphitheater where Glen is subdued and the fighting is done.

Men surround him and speak calmly, all seated. A council of elders has convened to decide his fate. Glen nods as they speak. He replies in kind as if reaching an agreement of peace.

I don't stop running, leaping, barreling across the large amphitheater to hear what he has to say for himself. I've heard plenty. I hurl myself at Glen's face. I'm huge now. My dick slaps the wind out of him. My chest heaves with glee.

He screams as I take a bite out of his cheek. Crushed beneath me, his fists fall on my unyielding bulk. He's helpless against my strength. I tear off his nose, spit away the gristly cartilage, and gulp down the rest. Chin and tender meat beneath the eye socket comes next, raw and warm. The baby is still hungry. I rip away his lips and tongue, and his howling takes on a less human tone. I give his fresh blood back to the land. Exceptionalism requires violence. We are exceptional. We are ravenous.

Hands and more hands upon me. The members of the Brotherhood pull and tug, but they can't stop me. I'm larger now, growing again, fleshing out on all fours as I snort and stomp upon Glen, whose screaming has already ceased.

I toss my massive head in the air and swing my horns at the heretics. I spin and charge, my hooves crushing chairs and men alike. Caught upon my horns, a naked gladiator becomes a smashed toy, limp and lifeless before he hits the ground.

Men scatter as I stampede.

Blood and the spilled juice comingle on the stage where I ascend. I flex my strong white flanks and swish my tail, snorting aggressively. Then I smash the apparatus on the altar. I fling the urn high into the rafters. It lands shattered behind me. The glass tubing and wooden bowls crack under my shining hooves. I am glorious. I kick the altar until it crumbles. I destroy my temple. I am free.

With ropes, stealthily, they creep up around me, men on all sides. Men with well-honed skills, and too many of them to charge at once, though I drive the first onslaught into the footlights and over the edge. I buck and rage as a rope loops around my horns. It tightens. Ten men pull, but they can't unseat me. Another lasso snags my back leg. The rebels pull from opposite directions, and then switch tactics. Their combined effort swipes my hooves out from under me. My great white heaving bulk lands on its side, smashing ribs, free legs kicking.

More ropes that tie my limbs, more men. I can't move. One of them approaches with a raised machete. He aims for my neck. All I can do is groan and squeal in bound protest.

The blade comes down. I'm on the curb at the crosswalk again, felled and prone. Across the street, the walking man icon blinks, the one with a jagged, rushing body and no circle for a head. Cars honk and rev impatiently as the voice from the signal speaker counts down the time left to cross. Ten, nine, eight. On the sidewalk below sits my lopped off human head, oozing and tilted, my eyes fixed on me.

I'm bleeding out. I pull my pregnant body over the asphalt. If I can put my head back, maybe I can stop the bleeding. Maybe I can think straight.

Seven, six, five, four. My strength is fading. Nothing makes sense. The gritty street resists my effort. I'm sprawled across two lanes, groveling, scratching my way across.

My head, if I don't reach it, will it sizzle into a small circular dot of light and be absorbed to complete the signal? Is that the meaning of my body, a symbol for public use, a sign and not the thing itself?

Three, two, one.

A stain on asphalt? I'm reaching, I'm pulling. I'm over the center dividing line. Angry drivers edge forward, daring the stoplight to deny them an inch. Exhaust pours over me in a flood. Tires, engines. My head, my head.

Zero.

The walking man icon turns red.

COMPANY POLICY

LARRY HINKLE AND VALERIE B. WILLIAMS

B *eep!*
The laptop harmonizes with beeps from medical monitors attached to the small body in the hospital bed. Annie's chest rises and falls, but her eyes remain closed. Rob Molnar reaches out to stroke his five-year-old daughter's head. The nurse had shaved the remaining clumps of hair from her head yesterday, at Annie's request. She said they looked dumb.

Annie has spent way too much time in hospitals lately. So has Rob. He'll always be there for her, of course, but he still has to work. Especially now. He knows firsthand he won't be able to get health insurance at a new job, thanks to Annie's illness. Guiltily, he moves his eyes from Annie to the computer screen.

Click. Log into the SafeHarbor Medical Insurance network. Click. Open the Elkins file. May as well start with an easy one—preexisting condition. He scans the page, making sure he hasn't missed anything they could use to reverse his decision. As he hovers the mouse over the Deny button, the hair on the back of his neck prickles, and a slight scent of sulfur and gunpowder floats in the air. He shivers from a sudden but familiar drop in temperature.

Rob places the laptop gently on the foot of the bed and turns around, his breath now a visible mist. Two shimmering figures, like holograms, hover there. And one is that bastard, Lindell.

Rob had seen his first ghost fifteen months ago, after celebrating his promotion to Regional Manager at SafeHarbor Medical Insurance. His intimate knowledge of medical regulations, and how to use them to the company's advantage, had saved SafeHarbor hundreds of thousands of dollars since he'd joined the company in 2005, so the promotion and accompanying raise was the least they could do. It took three years, but this was his first step up the ladder and he wouldn't let the opportunity go to waste.

With his new title came an office with a door and his own assistant. After moving his possessions from the cubicle farm, he slammed the door shut, causing the rest of the staff to pop their heads over the partitions like a mob of meerkats. He glared through the glass, and they slunk down into their seats.

He logged on to the network to deal with the next appeal in the queue. The paper trail, as usual, was solid—the staff followed his strict rules and their decisions had only been overturned twice in three years—but the fact that the policyholder had tried to manipulate his decision by including pathetic anecdotes and pictures with no relevant data annoyed him to no end. Insurance was a data-driven business, not a charity. Not on his watch.

A movement in the corner of the office caught his eye, and he raised his head. Rob blinked and looked again. The translucent form of a woman bobbed in the air, scowling. Was that…Moira Jennings? Rob gasped and rubbed his eyes. She was still there.

He got to his feet, backing toward the closed door and feeling for the doorknob. He turned it and slipped out of the room.

Moira had died last week from a rare form of cancer. Rob had denied her coverage for a non-FDA-approved treatment and had received an earful from her over the phone right before they transferred her to hospice. He'd told her he was terribly sorry, but the decision was out of his hands. Company policy, he explained. Who was he to argue with that? What he didn't tell her was that he wrote the policy in question.

Standing outside his office, he took a deep breath, then called for his assistant.

Evelyn scurried over, tucking wisps of hair back into her tight bun. "Yes, Mr. Molnar. What can I do for you?"

"Look in my office and tell me what you see."

Evelyn gave him a puzzled look, then peered through the door. If she'd heard the quiver in his voice, she didn't let on. "Umm, I see your desk, your computer, the rubber tree plant in the corner." She brightened. "Oh, I don't see your coffee mug. Would you like me to fetch you a cup?"

Rob stood behind her, looking over her shoulder. Moira Jennings still floated in the corner of the room. She crooked her finger and beckoned him back into his office.

"No, I need a break anyway. Just hold my calls for a few minutes."

He marched toward the employee lounge, looking back over his shoulder as he went. When he returned to his office twenty minutes later, the ghost was gone, but grunts and moans were coming from his computer. Someone had logged him onto a porn site! He slammed his laptop shut, then slumped in his high-back executive chair, heart pounding. What the fuck was going on?

Moira Jennings was the first ghost of a deceased client to haunt him, but not the last. Several others whose claims he'd denied also tormented him, including Benji Allman, a teenager who'd declined rapidly when his mother tried an unproven treatment in Mexico after being denied coverage for an expensive drug prescribed off-label. Rob couldn't understand why Benji was haunting him, since it was his mother's fault he was dead. Benji's gaunt form, veins visible beneath his paper-thin flesh, often floated over Rob's shoulder, watching him work. An odor, sickly sweet but sour underneath, followed in his wake. Rob imagined it was the smell of the cancer that killed him, eating away at his organs before they shut down for good. How had his mother put up with that stench? If you asked him, he'd done her a favor.

There were two other ghosts who accompanied Benji that Rob didn't recognize, but they were silent and mostly harmless, restricting their activities to blowing papers around on his desk. Nothing a few paperweights couldn't handle. As for Benji, after the third complaint to HR about the obscene music coming from his office—Benji liked to play hardcore rap on Rob's computer—Rob learned to keep a pair of headphones plugged into his laptop. Nobody asked why he never wore them.

He'd quizzed his employees many times, but temperature drops aside, he was the only one who could see or smell the hauntings. Evelyn had wrinkled her nose a few times upon entering his office, but that could have been from the multitude of air fresheners he kept plugged in. Just to be safe, he powered off his laptop whenever he stepped out of his office and locked the door behind him.

Such constant breaks in the flow of work put him behind, however, so he began to work at home more often, something he'd tried to do as little as possible after his wife had walked out on him two years ago. She'd always been a free spirit, and Rob's devotion to the almighty dollar was the root of all their problems. Eventually, not even her little girl outweighed their constant fighting, and she was gone. He hadn't heard from her since. Just as well, since the longer she was out of their lives, the more Rob appreciated being his daughter's sole parent. She adored him, and he adored her. Everything he did at work—the Draconian policies he wrote, the tough calls he made that no one else would, or could, and all the money that came with it— he did for her.

While his past decisions literally haunted him in the office, at home, he was more productive than ever. He'd nearly forgotten what it was like to work uninterrupted.

Until the night Roger Lindell showed up.

Rob had slipped out of Annie's room as usual, leaving the door cracked to let the light from the hallway in. He stood outside her room until he heard her breathing, slow and rhythmic, then went into the kitchen, where he poured himself two fingers of scotch. He carried his drink to the living room and opened his laptop.

The last week in the office had been rough. Rob had recently denied coverage for Roger Lindell's son because the doctors had prescribed an expensive drug off-label, a last-grasp alternative treatment after all other avenues had been exhausted. Distraught, Lindell had shot his son, then turned the gun on himself. Rob's assistant, Evelyn, had spoken to Lindell every time he called, stalling the desperate father and covering for Rob when he refused to deal with the man. After Lindell's murder/suicide, she'd spent the next three days moping around the office with pink-tinged eyes, like some sort of oversized albino rabbit. Did she blame Rob for their deaths on some level? He didn't care. Lindell pulled the trigger, not him.

Rob drained half his scotch in one gulp. He set the glass down on the coffee table, then logged onto the SafeHarbor network.

No sooner had he opened the first file when a wave of cold air rolled through the living room, accompanied by a slight whiff of gunpowder, which dissipated when the furnace kicked on. It felt like someone was watching him. He glanced toward the hallway, praying it was his daughter, but instead met the angry eyes of Roger Lindell's ghost.

His breath caught in his throat. "You, you… How did you get here?" His voice raised in pitch. No ghost had followed him home before. They hadn't dared. This was his sanctuary.

The laptop sparked, then the screen flashed to a video of a surgery in progress. The patient wasn't visible except for a shape under a sheet. A tiny shape. A high-pitched buzz sounded. The buzz changed tone when the surgeon pressed the surgical saw into the patient's skull. Rob pushed the laptop aside and covered his eyes. The whine of the bone saw continued, along with a horrible sucking as the assistant vacuumed blood and cerebrospinal fluid away from the incision. The dusty smell of blade through bone filled his nostrils. Sickened, Rob leapt to his feet and charged toward Lindell. He stumbled through the apparition and crashed into the wall. He pushed himself up to his feet, then retched. The back of Lindell's head was missing, destroyed when he'd put the gun in his mouth and pulled the trigger. Bits of bone and gore and brain matter ringed the exit wound.

Lindell slowly turned to face Rob.

"Make it stop!" Rob pleaded. "Please!"

Lindell snorted. "Why? This is the treatment that would have saved Sam, if he'd had the right drugs to shrink the tumor. But we never had the chance to find out because you denied him! It could've saved his life!"

"You don't know that." Rob ran his sleeve across his mouth.

"You're right, I don't. Thanks to you."

"It was company policy," Rob sputtered, lunging for the laptop on the couch. "Nothing I could do." He fumbled for the power button. The video stopped and Lindell disappeared. Rob spun, waiting for the ghost to reappear.

"Daddy? My head hurts." Annie's soft voice floated down the hallway.

Rob stood for a moment, getting his breathing under control. Annie didn't need to see him like this.

"Coming, honey." He ran his fingers through his hair, closed the laptop, and went to Annie's room.

More and more ghosts appeared at work, forming Rob's personal Greek chorus of misery. The dramatic temperature swings didn't happen with every haunting, but often enough that Evelyn called building maintenance on multiple occasions. Of course, they could never solve the issue.

Rob had insisted IT give him a new laptop, but it didn't make a difference. Neither did the second, third, or fourth time he demanded a replacement. Eventually, he realized it wasn't the laptop that was the problem; it was his job. Whenever and wherever he logged onto the SafeHarbor network, the portal between worlds opened.

But he found himself in a trap of his own making. Annie's headache the night Lindell showed up was the first of many, sometimes severe enough to make her vomit, the violent retching and screams of pain piercing Rob's heart. Her pediatrician thought it might be migraines, possibly inherited from her mother. The doctor said it would help if she could talk to Annie's mother about her family medical history, but Rob had no idea where his ex-wife was or how to get in touch with her. The prescribed medication seemed to help—until Annie had her first seizure. After a series of expensive tests that quickly fulfilled Rob's deductible, the doctors had a diagnosis: glioblastoma, an aggressive and serious brain tumor with only a 20% five-year survival rate.

They recommended treatment begin immediately. First, chemotherapy to shrink the tumor, hopefully enough for the surgeons to remove it. If that didn't work, radiation. Rob felt numb as he listened to everything the doctors wanted to do to his little girl. She was only five years old! How could her tiny body possibly survive? And if she did, what would it do to her spirit? The headaches and seizures had already reduced her to an echo of the cheerful child she'd once been.

Rob spent the month after Annie's diagnosis in and out of the hospital with her. The company was generous in giving him time off so he could focus all his energy on helping Annie. He daydreamed about starting fresh with a new job. But he knew it was only a fantasy. Annie was uninsurable anywhere else.

After that first month, his manager advised him that SafeHarbor was willing to let him work full-time remotely, if that's what he needed. He could even set his own schedule to accommodate hospital visitation hours.

He got the hint.

He spent his days at the hospital and his evenings at the computer, trying to ignore his tormentors and surviving on three or four hours of sleep a night. But he couldn't keep up with the workload, so one day he reluctantly brought the laptop to the hospital, hoping to sneak in some work while Annie slept.

"I s nothing sacred?" Rob whispers to the ghosts hovering in the hospital room. He sets his laptop on the end of Annie's bed. "Can't you see how sick she is?"

"You didn't care how sick my Sam was," Lindell says. "Pretty easy for you to hide behind your computer screens and forms and 'rules,' wasn't it? To avoid the pain and suffering your decisions caused. How does it feel now?"

"I told you, there was nothing I could do. It was company policy!" Rob clenches his fists so tightly the nails dig into his palms. Was all the money he'd made the company worth all this? He steeled his jaw. No, there was no room for doubts. No room for regrets. He'd done the right thing. It was just business, after all. Were their circumstances reversed, he's sure Lindell would have made the same decisions if it meant more money, more security, for his boy. Maybe he could appeal to Lindell's parental instincts and convince him to leave Annie out of it. If Lindell wanted to haunt him at home or in the office, fine. But his daughter, and her hospital room, should be off-limits.

He glances at Annie, still sleeping, and silently thanks the doctors for the strong pain meds they'd given her. He turns to Lindell. "I'm asking you, as a parent who's been through this, to leave her alone. This is between you and me. She has nothing to do with it." He lowers his head. "Please."

"The way you left us alone?" Lindell smirks. "With no way to pay for Sam's treatment? Your 'company policy' killed my boy!"

The other ghost, a woman Rob doesn't recognize, nods. She passes her hand through one of the monitors, and the beeping speeds up for a moment, then returns to normal.

"I didn't put the gun to his head," Rob says through gritted teeth. "Or in your mouth. You killed him! He might have pulled through, but you turned a possibility into a certainty."

"Sam's death was always a certainty, thanks to you. I only made sure he wouldn't travel alone. All of this," he spreads his arms and looks around the room, "is an unexpected bonus."

"So where is Sam? Why isn't he here torturing me, too?" Rob asks, putting bravado he doesn't feel into his voice. "Or did he end up traveling alone *after all?*"

For an instant, the ghost's face reflects sorrow and hurt. Satisfaction runs through Rob like an electric current. Good! He got to the SOB. But Lindell's anger and bitterness quickly return, and the moment of vulnerability is gone.

"Sam is at peace. I may join him, someday, but in the meantime you'd best get used to my company. And everyone else whose lives you've destroyed." Lindell's joyless smile never touches his eyes. "There are so many of us. So, so many. And not just the ones your personal decisions killed. Oh no. Those 'company policies,' the ones you wrote and your department enforced, led to multiple deaths. You'll never have another peaceful moment. Not on my watch."

As if on cue, Annie thrashes in her bed, back arching and fists flailing. The female ghost claps her hands as the beeps from the machines become more urgent. An alarm rings out. The room fills with medical personnel. "Jesus, why is it so cold in here?" one of them yells. Rob steps toward the bed and reaches for Annie's hand, only to be pushed aside.

He stands frozen, hand to mouth, as the medical team works to control her seizure. His laptop crashes from her bed to the floor, but Lindell's ghost still hovers next to him, watching the action as if at a sporting event. Rob scoops up the computer and disconnects the network, closing the portal between his office and here. Lindell and his silent companion disappear. But he knows they'll be back.

They always come back.

Rob holds his daughter's small hand and counts the number of times her chest rises and falls. Tubes and wires monitor her every bodily function. Last week's seizure had been the first of an escalating series, finally forcing the doctors to put her into a coma to allow her poor little body to rest.

He knows logging onto the network opens the portal, so he hasn't worked in the hospital since Annie took a turn for the worse last week. Lindell had been here then, taunting him. Were the two events related, or just a coincidence? The look of grim satisfaction that crossed Lindell's face while watching Annie suffer told him it was the former. After all, the first time Lindell had followed him home was the night Annie got sick. And that horrible brain surgery video! Rob shuddered at the memory. Poor Annie had undergone a similar surgery as part of her treatment. It was a standard operation, so his insurance covered it. Rob hadn't watched, of course, but the memory of the video tortured him during his hours in the waiting room.

A sharp knock at the door behind him snaps him back to the present. Before he can collect himself, Annie's neurologist Dr. Martinez strides into the room, followed by two fresh-faced interns carrying tablets.

"Good news, Mr. Molnar." Dr. Martinez flashes a smile. "We plan to bring Annie out of the coma over the next two days. She's stable and we should be able to control the seizures."

"That's great." Rob runs his hand through his unwashed hair. "What are our next steps?"

"Since we couldn't get the whole tumor with surgery, we have to try another way to shrink it. It's an alternative protocol, with some off-label drugs normally used for psychosis and strokes, but it's shown great promise."

Rob stops listening. There's no way SafeHarbor's policy will cover the treatment. He tunes back in when he realizes the doctor is asking him a question.

"So, do we have your permission to proceed?"

"Sorry, I missed part of that. If we don't use this treatment, what other options do we have?"

The doctor's eyes widen. "I'm afraid we are out of options, Mr. Molnar. But as I said, this protocol has been very promising. Don't let the words 'alternative' or 'off-label' scare you off."

Rob shakes his head. "My insurance won't cover it. What would it cost if I self-paid?"

Dr. Martinez looks shocked and murmurs a question to one of the interns. After tapping on the tablet for a moment, he turns the screen to face Rob.

Rob's jaw drops. Even if he cashed in his 401k and other investments, took out a second mortgage, and maxed out his credit cards, he could still never afford the treatment.

He strokes Annie's face and bows his head. "Could we go ahead and bring her out of the coma?" he asks. "Once she's awake, I'll let you know my decision."

"Of course. I'll send the nurse in to get started."

As soon as the room clears, Rob reaches for his laptop. He knows the policies better than anyone. If there's a loophole to cover the treatment, he'll find it. He doesn't look up when the nurse enters the room to inject the first of the drugs to bring Annie out of her coma. He barely flinches when Lindell appears, floating on the other side of Annie's bed. The nurse shivers and leaves, telling Rob she's going to call maintenance about the chill.

Rob's search becomes more frantic with the drop in temperature. He finds nothing. Nothing! The policy is tight as a drum. He should know. He'd written it, after all. He'd maximized the company's profits and earned himself a promotion, but at what cost?

Lindell chuckles.

"Lindell…" Rob stops typing, his shoulders slumped from exhaustion. "Here to gloat?" He raises his eyes to the wraith. "Please, leave us be."

The ghost shakes his head. "Oh, no. This is the good part." Lindell looks down at the dying child. "I know you think I take pleasure in her pain. That I'm somehow responsible for it." He meets Rob's eyes. "I don't. And I'm not. Her illness is simply karma for your actions, and the only pain I enjoy is yours. To me, to all of us, your misery is sweet nectar of the gods." Lindell floats over the bed and hovers next to Rob. "There is a way to end her suffering, you know. And yours." He lifts his hand and points a finger gun at Annie's head. "Bang!" he says. Next, he points at Rob's head. "Bang!"

Rob leaps to his feet, knocking the chair to the floor and dropping the laptop as he backs away. "No!"

"Come on, Rob. Be a man! Why make your daughter suffer any more than she has to? You know there's no hope, not with the way you wrote those health policies your company offers. Or should we call them 'death policies'?" Lindell's chuckle turns into a bitter laugh.

Unable to hold back any longer, Rob bursts into sobs so wrenching they blind him and steal his breath. By the time he recovers his composure, Lindell is gone. He picks up the laptop. The screen had cracked when he dropped it, but it's still on. The room temperature feels normal.

Annie stirs and opens her eyes. Rob rushes to her side and takes her hand.

"I'm here baby. Daddy's always here."

A nnie came out of her coma, but spent much of the next week in an opiate-induced haze to control the pain. Rob slept in her hospital room, when he could sleep. More often, he used the damaged laptop to continue searching fruitlessly for a loophole. Work piled up in his inbox. Mercifully, Lindell and the other ghosts stayed away. Rob hoped the damage to the computer had broken the portal between worlds, but he feared they were just biding their time.

Unable to afford the treatment or circumnavigate the policies he'd written, Rob made arrangements with hospice and took his daughter home to die.

The foreboding, sour smell he'd associated with Benji permeates his house now, no matter how many air fresheners and flowers he sets out.

He sits vigil at her bedside in her pink princess bedroom. An IV pump administers her pain meds on a schedule, but the hospice nurse had shown him how to inject a bolus into the line if she needed more. On just the second day at home, Annie begins to moan and thrash.

"Hold on, honey." He empties a syringe into the line and waits.

"Daddy! It hurts!"

He injects another syringe.

She screams and smashes her head against the bedrail, leaving a smear of blood.

He injects another syringe.

She quiets. Her breathing slows, then turns into gasps, with more time between each successive intake. Rob leans in, willing her to take that next breath. She inhales, then exhales. Inhales, then exhales. And then, nothing.

Rob's world ends with her.

"Why? Why her, God? It's not fair," he yells at the empty room, all the while clutching his daughter's body as if he could transfer his own life force into her. He can't wrap his mind around the fact that he'll never again hear her laugh, see her dance, listen to her read stories.

Rob holds Annie until his arms go numb. He lays her gently back on the bed. When the feeling in his fingers returns, he removes the IV line and places a Band-Aid over the puncture. The bandage has Elsa from *Frozen* on it, Annie's favorite character. He pulls the covers up to her chin. She could be sleeping.

Numb, he wipes the blood from the bedrail, then stumbles into the living room and calls hospice. The damaged laptop sits on the coffee table. He hasn't turned it on since coming home. Now, however, he has no choice. He'll have to appeal to his boss's better angels, but he thinks he can save his job. He has to, if he ever wants to see Annie again.

Rob logs onto the SafeHarbor network, and waits.

And waits.

And waits.

LIBERTY

HIS EDGES

DONNA J. W. MUNRO

He was breathing hard through the screen. Chest rising quick and sharp. A wheeze at the end that belied the hard work he'd done that day. So many sips of power taken by so many little magics. All for the public's good of course. But it was hard on his body.

I couldn't interfere. It was his burden to feel the pain of making. It was his gift to the Body Politic that his strength was ours.

Bless the Fathers in their wisdom.

"Is there… someone out there?" His voice was thready and weak as he asked. He always asked. It was strange. So many of the others faded away into a dream of sorts as their life was spent in each of the stages of use that their existence dictated.

I fought the urge to respond with some kind of comfort. Even with all of the training, I still couldn't think of him the way I thought of the others. They were just shapes behind the screen, breathing breaths either on their own or with the wind of the machines filling them. They were parts. Power cells. Even bio-calculators that the brightest Fathers used for storing their memories while they worked on delicate operations that required a cold heart and an unencumbered mind.

I knew because I'd been trained in the understanding.

Most citizens had no idea what happened when they turned in the Cyclers for civic use. They just knew their duty and the rewards that came from following the Father's mandates.

"Please, just a few words," he wheezed behind the curtain, each word a labor to pass through. Each breath he took seemed jagged and full of wet—a sure sign that he wasn't long term use rated. Donor parts maybe. A healthy liver or clean veins was in high demand in the head of the Body Politic.

I'd never seen it, but I heard from others who served that the Fathers and their families ate food swimming in its own bloody gravy. They drank some nights until the wine and the whiskey flooded their bodies and they had to be revived in clinic. So many needs for clean Cycler livers and hearts. The talk was delicious in the dormitory dark when those like me, proto-citizens, rested between shifts.

I was lucky.

Not like this poor male behind the screen.

I might rise one day if I worked hard enough. If I did my best to ease the path of the Fathers, they might notice and raise me up. It happened! I'd seen it.

Just yesterday, a matron who'd been waiting twenty years to promote had been called to the administration office. She'd been giddy with joy when it was her name over the sound system.

"Nori #8743, report to admin for reassignment," the box intoned above our long row of beds.

She leapt up, pulling on her thin robe and didn't bother to gather her few effects.

"Good luck, Nori," my bunk partner Jona whispered as she hurried past.

I stared at the hairbrush Nori had treasured set out carelessly on her bed. A present from one of the Father's wives for some or another holiday they celebrated. Nori had flounced off and left it and we were sure she'd come back for it. That and her little collection of notions she'd been collecting for as long as she'd served.

"Jona, she forgot—"

"She'll be back."

But she hadn't come back all night. We didn't talk about it and had to believe that where she went there were such finer things that all her buttons and glass and her hairbrush were useless junk. Replaced as easily as the Fathers replaced failing organs and broken bones. Best not to think about it until it was my turn.

I scratched away on the report, taking down the Cycler's heart, breath, and temp vitals as I'd been trained. That day, he'd lent his processing power to the grid, keeping the living quarters of the uppers and the free folk aligned with their needs, turning lights on and off as they walked through the long halls that Nori had described. Not like the Five Hundreds that regulars worked in: a bedroom and a waste flush for bathing and purging, a chiller and micro to warm the gov-pouch protein allotment for their day.

"Are you… real?" The cycler's voice had more power behind each word. His nutrients must have been washing through his cells restoring some of what the day had spent. He was a special one, this cycler. He'd been here longer than any other I'd observed and seemed to have a whole lot left to give.

I cleared my throat, a bit too loudly. I couldn't say any words to him, but sounds were expected. Encouraged.

"I know you're out there. I can hear you." It was a murmur, but the tone of his voice had taken on a sonorousness that it often did once I'd taken over a shift. He seemed to like me, though I didn't make any note of that. What did such a feeling matter when, strong or not, he'd be gone after a few more cycles, silent or parts. It's the way with all cyclers.

"I know you can't talk to me, but… You always listen. I can tell that you…care?" His voice raised in a question, like I might argue with his ridiculous assertion. I took a spare reading of his vitals and penciled them in with extra loud strokes.

His heart had steadied and his breath was in parameters for rest, but some of his chem readings were in the upper ranges of normal. Readings I didn't understand but would write down for my betters. The Docs, like the Fathers, had more, did more, expected more and didn't have to give a worker like me anything other than the curt instructions and portions of nutrients that went along with my job.

"You sound different than the others," he said. "Nicer. Do you know what that is? I know you were lab grown and all."

Sometimes he said things I didn't know how to interpret and ached to ask about. "Lab grown" is what all humans were. How else would we be made? The way he talked and the words he used, all cyclers used, sounded like they were sideways in my ears. They talked about mothers and cooking. They mumbled about dirt. Strange things that I had never heard inside the complexes and labs that humanity lives in.

I wanted to ask, "What are you really?" and "Where are cyclers from?" All I knew was that regular citizens turned them in whenever they found them inside our mirrored walls. The rewards were enormous. Extra portions, rec tokens, and access to revita-baths for aching muscles. Besides, one cycler was a month of ease. No work.

Nothing sounded better, though where I worked, I'd never see a cycler. They only managed to catch them in the lowest levels, the power plant and water tech levels below twenty.

This one said he'd been trying to get some medicine for his... sister, another word that didn't make much sense.

"I wish they would let me see you. Is it just part of the punishment? Keeping us behind frosted glass like fish or something."

Fish?

Every time I sat with him, he did this. It felt like the erosion I'd seen in the other cyclers only in me. They wore down with the demands of the Body Politic, serving a purpose only they could. This felt like he was wearing *me* down. Taking apart what I knew piece by piece only instead of falling apart, it felt like he was shining a light on what was already missing.

Those words he said stirred something. A need to know. It was so hard to keep quiet even with the camera watch lights blinking from every angle. I coughed lightly and paused in my writing.

"Is it worth it?" That's what he asked every night before he gave up talking and lapsed into a gloomy silence and passed into the soft, fitful sleep that a power cycler was allowed between shifts.

Is it worth it?

I'd never answer him, but his questions lodged in me each day. They came to me when I was trying to sleep or when I waited for my check-ins with the dorm admin. His questions made me look closer. They disturbed my trust.

Last night, I'd been pondering him when the admin took Jona back for her decomp session after her shift and I moved forward to the first seat by the door waiting my turn. Through the wide gaps, I heard her report all her data, her impressions, her thoughts without the reserve that I'd been growing ever since I'd first been paired with my current cycler, the man breathing behind the screen and thinking about me.

I was sitting there in the office, wondering if I'd omit any of my stranger, personal data like I had for the past few nights when I glanced over at the bin behind the dorm admin's desk. The things inside were to be incinerated, old gowns, worn out pumps and tools—all the things that normally should be destroyed with the night's clean up. What lay under that top layer of material caught my eye and my breath.

Nori's hairbrush.

The handle stuck out from between the folds of what might have been her old gray shift. I couldn't let them send her treasure to the fires because Nori might want it. I couldn't believe she'd want it destroyed no matter what she'd achieved in promotion, so I hurried over to snatch it out before the trash crew came through.

As Jona repeated the pledges of our job and satisfied the decomp process, I saw a bit more. A scrap of paper with Nori's name on it. Something that looked like her handwriting. I snatched it up and stuffed it along with her brush into the deep pocket of my over-jacket, then sat back in my seat to wait my turn with a thundering heart and sweat dotting my brow.

Control, I thought. Calm.

Calm because I didn't want the admin to know I was nervous. Guilty of the worst crime...questioning my betters. Part of me shuddered with the anxiety we'd learned to feel about thoughts that were poison to the Body Politic. No questions, no lies, no wants, no needs. We were taught to feel traitorous thoughts in our guts as needles and grit. But when I thought about the cycler's question—Is it worth it—something even deeper than my guts banged with a sharp retort.

Jona came out of the decomp with a neutral smile and untroubled brow. I tried to imitate the look as I got up and crossed into the admin's office myself.

She sat behind a desk piled high with notes from the watchers of our dorm. Though the piles seemed haphazard and unorganized we'd always been assured that our work was meaningful. She stretched out her hand and fluttered her fingers at me. My reports. I tapped them straight against the closest edge of the desk and passed them to her with care. She didn't look up from her own work as she plopped the set of forms on top of the nearest pile.

"This cycler of yours seems to be holding his power longer than predicted. Do you have any insights?"

I'd never been asked such a question before. Usually it was ranges and data. This was... my opinion? I wasn't supposed to have one. I stayed silent, hoping the admin would find some other thing, some less dangerous-feeling question for me. I let my fingernails bite the skin of my palms but kept my face placid. Quizzical.

"Well?"

I had opinions, but they were dangerous. He was fighting, challenging me and the work he had to do and maybe that's what made him last longer. Maybe the cyclers were stronger than us. This was mind poison and I knew it.

I tilted my head like I didn't understand and responded with, "His vitals are all within expected parameters. The influx of sleep med seems to take an average of five minutes longer than with most, but he sleeps. Breathing and temp–"

"I can read." The admin got up from behind the paper-piled desk and came close enough that I could see the tight weave of her gray smock. How fine and soft it looked. And I could smell her. There was a fragrance sweeter than our soaps in the dorm. "We are interested in this cycler. He has more power in him than the others, though we've noticed a better stock being brought in in the last few weeks. He is the strongest of them. The order is that we should try to talk to him. We see him trying to talk to you. We want you to encourage him. Write down all he says. Report to me each shift start and I will give you questions to ask and then at the decomp, you will come give us your impressions."

"Impressions. I'm not qualified–"

"Do this and you will be lifted to admin. You are cleared for this." Then she handed me a paper on top of my new clip of report pages for the next shift. "Practice these questions tonight. Try not to sound frightened when you ask them. It will become easier as you work."

All I could do was nod and scurry out with the papers clutched in my hand and Nori's brush in my pocket. I was to be raised like her only by doing work we'd been told was against the Body Politic. It didn't make sense.

I tucked myself into the single stall bathroom of the dorm knowing I'd only have a few minutes before one of my dormmates would need a moment to herself. I scanned the questions they gave me... just three. What's your name? How do you feel? Why did you come? Simple enough. Like Admin had advised I whispered them to myself, tasting the strangeness, the intimacy of questions I'd only ever asked my bunkmates. I closed the papers and pulled Nori's brush and the paper I'd taken from my pocket to look at.

The brush was just as I remembered, and it still had a few wiry strands of brown hair woven in the bristles from Nori's usually neatly plaited hair. The wildness of the strands made me catch my breath. How had I never seen her hair down in the years we'd been friends?

I set down the brush before it led me further into the well of sadness I'd discovered by touching Nori's treasured brush. The paper I'd found had Nori's name written at the top, but the rest of what was on the page beneath was a blocky set of lines constructed of symbols I'd never seen before.

I folded the paper tight and stuffed it into my undersuit, put the brush back in my pocket, and straightened out my shift just as another dormer rapped on the door. I flushed and opened the door, mumbling a greeting as I shifted past. The fluttery unease lay deep in my belly as I thought about saying words to the cycler, about where to hide Nori's note, and about what it would mean to advance to admin if I could. The promise of a Five Hundred pod whirled in my head. Privacy for the first time. The gnashing worry that someone could find the brush and use it to demote me ice-picked through the greed. And to talk to my cycler? The longing at the possibility mixed all the strangeness inside into a soup of sweaty worry.

"Are you good?" Jona's voice asked from the edge of the top bunk. She'd been asleep when I crept in and hadn't seen the Brush thank the Fathers. She'd have asked too many questions and I couldn't put her at risk like that.

"Yes," I whispered and turned over so she wouldn't ask me anything else.

Secrets are dangerous things in a dorm. They poison the air and whisper out through dream gilded lips. Secrets are like little treasures that others covet and want to have as their own. Even friends couldn't be given the breath that filled them, because they'd breathe them in for themselves to be more powerful. Turn you in for rec coupons. A secret reported was as good as finding a fresh cycler if it had enough precious breath in it.

I couldn't lose Jona to a secret.

I heard her roll in her own bunk above me, then in the quiet, I finally did fall away into my tangled up dreams.

The time awake before my shift passed quickly. Cleaning, listening to the teachings of the Fathers, pledge and promise, then it was time to report for my shift with the cycler. As I passed the admin nodded and I knew from the look on her face that this strange duty I'd been given weighed on her as much as me. Maybe up the chain there were secret promises being made. Threats couched in kind words. Razored hopes we all kept hidden in purposeful work.

"Is it worth it?"

His constant question dogged me as I gathered up all the report pages I'd need for the day. I entered the watching room and flicked on the light, then gasped as I took in the lack of a screen. There was no separation between me and him. No frosted window to keep me from seeing his features or the shape of his limbs under the starched sheet that covered most of him.

The sheeves of reports slid out of my grasp as I locked my gaze on his eyes. Blue. Shocking, bright blue nearly electric in the brightness of them. Browned skin with a sort of indeterminate set of features. Were the sorter to come and try to classify his genetic heritage, I didn't think he'd be classifiable without a blood panel, but the effect was…something quite new.

Not the conventional beauty that some of the uppers played in the rec hall soapgandas. Those white on white-on-white delicate folks nearly blinded me as they play acted what life was like for those who did right and good for the Body Politic. That beauty was so distant from my own brown hair and eyes, that I'd never even thought of the soapganda folks as the same kind of human as me. Same with the Fathers who were so tall and ruddy, filled with the parts of cyclers and as old as the world. No, this cycler's eyes stunned me with their clarity. The softness of their stare even as he was pinned to that bed and sweating from his day as a Fathers memory receptacle.

"You look like one of us," he said, marvel spilling out of his chapped, cracked lips.

From his weak smile, I knew that he was complimenting me. Though I ought to feel insulted that a cycler thought we were somehow alike in any way, I blushed a bit. I had to focus. I could move out of the dorm if I did this right. Move up in the ranks and maybe get one of the Five Hundreds with my own toilet and chiller. I set my face in a pleasant but distant sort of smile and took all his vitals.

"Why do you think they removed the screen this time?" He asked even though I hadn't spoken yet. Maybe just hearing a voice, his own even, helped him to stay strong enough to withstand the cycler's burden for the Body Politic.

I wasn't supposed to answer, but the question's possibilities flirted with the meat of my mind. I didn't know why, but I had guesses. The best one was that he'd feel more comfortable and willing to spill out answers to my questions as they came. I looked enough like him, true enough, and that alone might get him talking.

Not that he'd ever held back on talking before.

I settled in the chair, still centered in the adjacent room. I didn't have orders to go any closer to him. Besides, something about cycler rooms felt taboo. Like the forbiddenness of them was concentrated in that set of walls. To break through the plane between them, even without the frosted glass wall, felt dangerous.

I took a deep breath to settle my nerves and started my questions. "What's your name?"

He gasped a little at the sound of my words. I didn't look up from my papers to see the impact my words had on his expression, because my own face flushed with excitement.

It took a minute, but he told me, "James. James of 98th."

I scribbled down what he'd said, wondering over the whole name. James. I'd never heard that name before. I wanted to say it to myself and test its edges, but I hadn't been given permission. The second half had to be some kind of place or level designation. My second name was Dormer and would change to Admin if I moved up as promised.

"What's your name?"

I shook my head. I couldn't give that to him without permission, but I longed to. It felt like an exchange of promises that I couldn't keep, so I just pressed on into the next question.

"How do you feel?" I asked.

This time I glanced up, curious to see how he looked as he took stock. His gaze met mine and I felt it the way that I felt the rush of energy after a revite bath. He was so thin: he looked like he was all edges and angles, but there was power in the set of his eyes.

"I'm okay. Is that what they want me to say? Do they want a list of all of my complaints? The way it felt when one of your asshole leaders crammed his mind into mine, pushing aside all of my thoughts, so he could do whatever atrocity he had lined up for the day?"

His words cut me and I didn't write them. They seemed too angry to be of use. I studied his face and it closed like a door, guarding whatever thoughts hid behind.

"What's your name?" He asked, voice harder this time.

I cleared my throat and took a calming breath. "Why did you come?"

"What's your name?"

He stared at me, gaze as unyielding as I'd ever seen. I wasn't supposed to share my name. I wasn't told to do it.

"Please… Why did you come?"

"What's your name?"

"I… can't." I scratched a nervous pattern in the margin of my first report.

The silence stretched between us and we breathed in time with each other. I dared a glance at him and his gaze still held me like a prisoner. He wasn't going to answer me. Somehow I knew that question was a step too far without some kind of a vouchsafe promise. Words so precious that he might be able to trust me.

Why not give him a name?

"Alicona Dormer."

My voice seemed to echo in the space between us the way footfalls did in the dorm at night, louder than possibility or truth.

"Alicona," he said back. "Sounds like Alice from home."

"So why did you come?" I tried again, not wanting to stray too far from the assigned questions.

He laid back on his cot and pulled the thin sheet back up to his brown shoulders. "Goodnight, Alicona. May your work be worth your spent breath."

He closed his eyes and I knew there'd be no more answers this night. As I shuffled together my reports, so many more words and questions danced through my mind, but I swallowed them.

I needed to remember the promise of the Admin. A better life. A better position. The promise to climb. I walked away without looking back, but the echo of his last words made me want to sound my breaths.

N ew questions came each day, always about his work and how he reacted and why he came.

His answers to those canned questions became...monotone. The silences stretched and he lay still, eyes closed, as distant as he ever had been with the screen up between us. Maybe more because he wasn't asking me questions.

"Is it worth it?" That is all he asked.

"H ere are the new questions." Admin barely looked up when I came to decomp anymore. She didn't want to know anything from me about his vitals or his health. She didn't even ask for the answers to the questions she'd asked the night before.

"How much longer will I be required to do this?" I had started having long nights of reliving how his body was changing, how his voice was thinner, how he didn't always see me. How he was finally beginning to sink under the weight of his work for the Fathers and the Body Politic.

She didn't answer my question with words. Instead, she handed me another pile of report papers she'd added to the massive pile on her desk at the end of the day. "You may choose to ask any questions you'd like or to respond to his questions freely. I can't tell you how long this will go on, but I will tell you," she checked a report on her desk written in the scrawl that the scrap of Nori's report had on it, "Your Nori is to be your Five Hundred pod mate. She shares the adjoining wall with the room set aside for you."

Nori! Just the thought of seeing her again and maybe slipping her her treasured hairbrush, hugging her and whispering how freeing it had been to talk to James, being safe in the next level with her friend—it all swirled together in a strange lovely breathy mix, tinging through her like what she imagined a kiss would be if she had that privilege.

Maybe she'd even earn that.

"We want to encourage this one to live, Alicona. Do your best with him." Admin turned her back and I knew it was time to go.

I hurried through eating my pouch and the steam shower, then to bed. If I could get him talking again, then–

"Why are you so happy all the time," Jona asked, dropping off the top bunk to sit beside me. We had a few minutes until lights out and lately Jona hadn't been spending them with me. She'd been distant and quiet, so I was glad to have a turn back to normal.

"I guess it's because I'm happy with my work right now."

Jona stared at my face with narrowed eyes, studying me for long seconds. "I've heard things, Alicona. Like you are getting special treatment for some reason. People say you are with Admin for twice as long as anyone else. They say your gov-pouches are fuller than ours."

Of course the other dormers would notice. What else did they have but routine and when it broke... Jona had always been a friend, my closest since we'd come out of the protocitizen growth centers together. I owed her an explanation. I owed her truth more than anyone else.

"I'm on a special assignment now. It's just... more work."

"Like doing what?"

"Promise you won't tell the others? I don't know what Admin will do if I—"

"Promise."

I took a deep breath and leaned closer so the next bunk's occupants wouldn't hear. "I have to ask mine questions. He's named James and he's lived twice as long as the others. I guess they want to figure out why."

Jona threw her arms around me and whispered right into my ear, "Be careful. Those cyclers are full of poison thoughts. Remember the Fathers..."

"Saved us from their pollution. Made us pure. I know. Don't worry. I just ask my questions and report the answers."

Silence hung between us for a few seconds.

"I wonder if they are scary... you know, looking. Or if they eat each other? You know, monsters like in the lessons from the growth center."

I shrugged. "I haven't had to ask." I knew he didn't because I'd looked into his eyes and seen nothing but kindness, worry, and pain. And scary looking? He looked like us.

"Is it worth it?" His words echoed in my exhausted brain.

The next day, I tucked Nori's hairbrush and the scrap of paper about her into my smock, safe from the dorm flip clean between sleep shifts. I ate my bigger Gov pouch quickly, knowing it was noted by my friends, then headed off to sit with James.

He lay under the sheet breathing fitfully in a thin sleep. His eyes darted under the thin tan skin of his eyelids and his hair fell back from his forehead in soft short waves. I'd come to think of him as quite beautiful in the time I could see him without a screen obscuring him, edges and dark skin and all. He was more than most of us. Even trapped here with the program wires and inputs pressed into his skin, his form vibrated with a life I'd never experienced before.

I put my reports down on my chair and walked to the edge of his space where the screen had once separated us from each other. The ghost of the line still haunted the floor, a physical change between my concrete and his steel, slightly concave floor. How bright white the room was. Sterile for his safety. Sharp and full of edges but cold. My hand reached out and brushed his bony, bare shoulder. His edges warmed the pad of my fingers. His edges weren't supposed to be. He was vital and full when he got here. Curved with muscle and potential that the Fathers used.

The old prayer flirted with my thoughts. Bless the Fathers and their wisdom, but it wasn't the blessing of it that brought it to my mind. It was the questioning of it. Was it worth it?

"Good morning, Alicona." His bright eyes had opened and were full of me. The thought of it thrilled me, even as I scuttled back from him into my own space.

"Good morning, James. How are you today?" Not quite the suggested question, but I had permission, and I was going to use it.

"Tired. The things they make me do… I thought our elders were telling fairy tales when they said things about the skyscraper enclaves. It's all true and worse." He pulled himself up, wincing with the effort. *Still strong enough to move,* I wrote on my report automatically. My mind was on his words.

"What's a skyscraper enclave?"

He laughed bitterly. "You don't know because they don't tell the help."

The help. His voice held a sneer when he said it. Wasn't helping the Body Politic good? It's what she'd always known. Her life would be one of help and maybe if she did well, she'd be promoted through the layers higher and higher and maybe someday, like Nori, she'd be on the track to full citizenship. Help was the only way.

"We are told things," I said, trying to keep my voice modulated from showing the hurt.

"I've seen you looking at a paper before, but not being able to read it. Why can't you?" His voice sounded confident, like he already knew.

"We dormers learn the short hand of entry so that we can efficiently report to the Admin of our dorms. There's no need for us to learn regular and upper script. They'd just clutter our minds."

"I can read it, if you want me to," he said.

I couldn't stop the gasp that split my primly set mask. How would a cycler know such a precious thing?

"I'm going to trust you, Alicona. I know you are here to spy, but I know you don't tell them everything." He whispered and I wondered why, but I saw his gaze darting to the corners of his room and understood. The uppers were watching. They had to be.

"When they press their memories into my mind like I'm some kind of bio-hard drive, I learn. You can't tell them that though. They'll kill us both." He said. "I can read their fancy upper writing."

The thought of harboring this information was traitorous. Part of my mind screamed at me that I was a proto-citizen with a duty to report. But another part of me knew that something wasn't lining up between our realities. Which was right?

"Press it into my hand while you pretend to take a manual pulse. Let me see it. I'll tell you what it says."

My stomach turned with worry. If I did this thing, I'd be a traitor. Every Gov-pouch I ate, every hour I logged in my bunk, every steam shower would be theft from the Body Politic.

Would it be worth it?

As my body trembled with the weight of my thoughts, my hand reached deep into my pocket and fingered the thin slip of paper. I had to know. Just this thing. None of the other things that might sit waiting behind those bright eyes.

I pulled it out and said in my regular voice, "Let me check your pulse, James."

I passed him the slip of paper and retreated to my chair to scrawl down the number. Elevated. He was just as excited by my trust as I was by his knowledge.

It felt like leaping off a ledge and flying, even if I'd smash into the forbidden outside streets. It felt right.

He tucked his hand down under his sheet and the movement wobbled his wires and sensors enough that I had to note the discrepancies. It was a marker the Admin could go back to look at if I wasn't careful. A cough is what I recorded. A lie that wouldn't set off any alarm bells. Cyclers often coughed as they gave their strength to their jobs. Coughed, cried, vomited, and sometimes, blood came out of their noses and mouths. It would be deemed normal.

I'd lied officially this time.

"Tell me about your life, Alicona. If you do, tomorrow I'll tell you all you want to know about mine."

Hours of explanations about the Body Politic, the Fathers, the laws and rewards, the dorms and Five Hundreds, about Jona and Nori and how we rose or froze based on our efforts, the training at the growth center where we'd been cultured and hatched passed with him asking a few questions, but mostly lying in the light of the room listening. I felt the eyes of admin through the corner cameras of the room, and I wondered if this was what they wanted or if I had gone too far.

It is not a proto-citizen's lot to question the Fathers or our admin. It is ours to do and give.

I told him that, too, though he scoffed at the words and I felt… ugly for the first time in my life.

"Alicona, there's nothing I can say that will convince you if everything you've said is what you believe, but this life," his eyes were open now, staring at me with all the blue full of fire and life, "this life of yours is a lie."

The machines next to him whirred to life for the first time in days, pumping him full of the yellow juice that put him to sleep. He fought it as his eyelids grew heavy.

"Come back," he said, struggling to keep his eyes on me. "Come… back…"

Then he was out.

I sat quietly and listened to his labored breaths for a while, clutching my half-filled out reports on my lap. Saying all those things that were part of my life and watching his face contort made me question so many things. Why would that be his reaction to who we were? If things were so bad outside, why would he have such revulsion about our well-worn systems? Part of me thought, of course he'd be disgusted. He was an outsider. He lived in the filth and was only half a human anyway. That part echoed all we'd been taught about the cyclers and their low way of being. But the part of me that had grown so much since he'd come, that part saw with his eyes.

That part wanted to know so much more.

I got up and left him, heading to the admin to turn in my reports and get ready for my sleep cycle. What would he tell me about his life tomorrow? Dark clouds swirled around that possibility. I knew this was dangerous. That somehow the knowing could be hurtful, but what could I do? It was what the Fathers required.

I took a deep breath before walking into the admin's office. Think Five Hundreds, think Nori, think about rising up. It ran through my head that all I should care about were those things. My future. But even as I ran those through my head, something inside panged with a hunger deeper than any time I'd been made to skip my gov pouch protein.

"Thank you for today," Admin said, taking my reports and putting them atop the tall pile on her desk. Though her words said one thing, her face said another. It was stone. Full of some bitterness that she carefully stowed. "The Fathers say you have done enough. Tomorrow, you will ascend to the Five Hundred and Jona will take over with him. You will train her, introduce her. All eyes will be on you."

I nodded and noticed a paper on her desk with my name on it. Other than that, I couldn't read the paper, but it looked just like the paper I'd fished out of the rubbish that was about Nori. The same as the paper the cycler had in his sheets.

I nodded. "Thank you, Administrator."

She waved me away.

I went through the rest of the evening like a dissociated cycler on his last day. I barely ate, passing the gov pouch across the table to Jona. I took a steam bath and thought about how it felt to explain our ways. How out loud, the things we did didn't even sound like they fit together right.

Something was missing and I hadn't even seen it before he'd started talking.

Is it worth it?

I didn't think it was.

I pretended to sleep until the dorm was full of soft snores and mumbles. When I stood, I checked on Jona. As much as I loved my friend, she'd tell the admin I was out of my bed in a second if it meant more pouches or a decomp session. That was just the way of things.

I don't know why I did it, but I took Nori's brush from under my own pillow and tucked it gently under Jona's so she'd find it. Maybe she'd understand if everything went wrong. Maybe she'd start thinking when she sat beside him in the morning, even if I wasn't there.

I made my way out and past the watchers, the cameras, and the admin's room into the hall. Cool and dark, I stuck to the shadowed side under the camera's view.

"Alicona?" He said as I came in.

"Yes. They want to replace me with Jona tomorrow. They say they are sending me up to the Five Hundreds."

He struggled under the bed sheets a bit. "Come close, Alicona."

When I did, he pulled the paper from under the sheet and passed it back to me. "I promised I'd tell you what this is. This paper is a requisition order for goods."

"What do you mean? It has Nori's name at the top of it. I can read that much. Are you sure you know the upper's language?"

He nodded, eyes full of something shimmering and awful. "This says Nori was reassigned from service to gov pouch production. It calls her protein. Do you understand what that means?"

My guts dropped inside my middle. It couldn't be. We weren't animals like the outsiders. We were advanced. We lived inside and bathed. We were… better. It couldn't be.

"Nori was reassigned to the Five Hundred. They took her up and gave her a living pod with its own micro and chiller. They rewarded her with—"

"They got rid of her. It says she aged out of service. She was made into protein for… it says here…the dormers nutritive needs. Do you understand?"

I did.

"There's a paper just like that on my admin's desk with my name. I'm supposed to train Jona and then they will elevate me to the Five Hundred tomorrow."

He shook his head. "You have to run, Alicona."

"Where? Where should I run to? There's only up or down. I—"

"Outside. You have to find my people. Run through the lowest floor. Follow the blue pipe's arrows. Don't stop for anyone."

"I can't. What about Jona?"

He shook his head. "She's not ready. She won't understand."

I knew that would be true. As much as she loved me, she'd turn me in for a decomp and a month off. It was an honor to do it.

I leaned in and grabbed his hand. "What about you?"

He smiled so full of sadness I didn't know what to do other than squeeze his hand.

"I'm dying, Alicona. Nothing's going to stop that. If I can free you from this, then I'll be glad to have been here. When I was young, the skyscraper enclaves all sent out raiders. My parents told me they stole all the girls they could find to come work. They took my baby sisters. Da said they raided out like that once a generation and only took the littles so they wouldn't know where they came from."

He coughed and groaned as the pain seemed to ripple through his body like a wave, making him curl up and clutch around my hand.

"My name is Adam Lincoln of the free Manhattan tribe. I feel like shit, Alicona. Like I've been squeezed out bottom to top by your damned Fathers and their demands for bio power and computing space. I came because I wanted to see if there were Manhattan sisters trapped here. I wanted to know if there was a way in and a way out. I wanted to send my tribe information about this damned place so they could save our sisters. Those are the answers your Fathers kept asking for and I'm giving them to you before they kill me. I want to send you to my people, Alicona. You can be my message."

I sobbed. I'd never even been off this floor before. My whole life had been pod nursery, training, dormer, and now the promise to move up to the Five Hundred. The lie of up.

Is it worth it?

"I'll do it."

"Here are the words you need to give the tribe when they find you at the end of the long pipe." He whispered the words I needed to give them so they wouldn't think I was a raider and try to kill me on the spot. "The light will be bright there. Brighter than you've ever seen. It will hurt for a while, but it's real."

I kissed him on the forehead. "Goodbye, Adam Lincoln. I'm sorry to leave you."

He pushed me away weakly and laughed. "You take me with you on the inside, Alicona. Now, go."

I 'd run from him and down the long hallway, trying to avoid as many of the camera eyes as I could. The path took me back past the pouch hall, the admin office, the steam showers, the nursery, and the dorm. At the end of the hall was a door I'd never thought of using since I knew it took me to the lowers. We'd never go down in the building. Every training, every teaching said up was the only way!

I put my hand on the door and pushed, but as it opened someone grabbed my arm.

"What are you doing, Alicona? Do you want to get us all in trouble?" Jona hissed behind me.

I turned and saw the care in my friend's wide eyes. She wanted to save me. Everything she'd been taught said that I must be having a breakdown.

"I'm sorry, Jona." My mind raced. She didn't know what I did. She hadn't heard about Nori or the other place. She wasn't about to be requisitioned for food. "I have to do this."

"You are to go up to the Five Hundred tomorrow. Why would you risk that?" Jona tugged at me.

"Come with me, Jona. Come see why I have to leave."

She knew me. Trusted me. We had been together all our years, from pod to bunk. That's the only reason she didn't scream for an admin right off.

"Just come. Believe in me, sister," I said to her, a whispered hope from my heart to hers.

Jona let me tug her into the doorway and down the stairs that spiraled, gray and dark. She was rigid in my grip, but she didn't resist. The concrete stairs gave way to metal and the passage opened up into a room full of pipes and vats and smells so awful I couldn't step forward until I'd gotten used to them.

"What is this?" Jona whispered, pressed up against my back, shaking.

I didn't know what to tell her, but the blue pipe with little red arrows along its belly hung right over our heads. I tugged her and we began to walk along the path it indicated. The vats were full of churning liquid next to us and as we walked, I realized that the slurry of protein we ate was cooking in each vat. I dreaded what had to be coming, but maybe this would be the thing that helped Jona understand. The vats were shoulder high and at this end, the slurry was the smooth paste we knew, ready to be packaged in the pouches for storage.

But the next vat was thinner. Not done cooking. Larger chunks floated on the surface, hunks of fatty pink and brown meat bubbled to the top and tumbled back down into the liquid, bits breaking off and churning around the surface.

As we passed that one and followed the blue pipe to the next, we saw a chute lower to the lip of the vat. First, clear liquid sloshed down the silver surface, half filling the vat in seconds. Then, thick brown liquid brought it up to three quarters full. Finally, as we were as close as we'd get to the vat the final ingredient tumbled down the chute and Jona gasped in my ear as she understood.

A leg, chopped into three sections and still bloody tumbled down, then two arms with hands still attached, then a head, features set in terror, splashed on the surface. Then another bloody, dismembered body. A woman like us, browner than the uppers, old like Nori, and chopped up to fit slid down. My feet anchored and my stomach turned, but we stayed and watched another five people fall into the now boiling vat which shifted forward the way we'd come and was replaced by another steel vat, filled the exact same way.

"That happened to Nori," I said to Jona. "And that's what they do to everyone they promise the Five Hundred to."

"No. It's a mistake," Jona said, but she let me lead her further into the gloom.

The passage went on and on, and behind me Jona sobbed. She stumbled. I told her what Adam had said. I told her what the outside would be like.

All she said was, "No."

She'd understand when we got there. She'd be glad I freed her when she didn't have to live in fear anymore.

DONNA J. W. MUNRO

The pipe led us deeper into wet, stinking places, then it turned and took us up a steep set of stairs. Eventually, what seemed like days later, we were at an opening where the light streamed in so bright I couldn't help but weep. Jona tried to run back but stumbled there in the entrance.

"Who are you?" A booming voice asked.

All I could see was shadows looming up. Ten, twenty. So many. So much bigger than us!

"I'm Alicona. I'm from the skyscraper complex. That's Jona. Adam Lincoln sent me."

"Adam?" A woman's voice asked, sounding strangled. "Is he dead? Where is he?"

"He's dying," I said. "But he sent me...us. He said I was to help you. To prove that the...taken were still alive."

"My Adam," the woman screeched. "She could be a spy. A liar. What proof does she bring?"

Jona crawled up next to me and clung to me. "Let's go back. We can still go back. They'll forgive us."

"You saw the vats, Jona. I can't do it."

"The words?" One of the men asked.

I thought about Adam's clear eyes. His kindness. How he'd been made to serve the Fathers and the uppers and how many of these people, people like me were just part of the disposable flesh the uppers relied on.

"He taught them to me, though I don't understand them all. They feel...important."

"Say them and we will explain them," the woman said, squatting down to look me in the face. "If Adam gave them to you, I will be your teacher. For him."

I nodded.

"We hold these truths to be self-evident, that all men are created equal, that they are endowed by their Creator with certain unalienable Rights, that among these are Life, Liberty and the pursuit of Happiness," I said, trying to get all the ways the words had worked in his mouth, right.

Jona looked at me with a strange sort of horror in her eyes. What I'd said were outlawed things, though we'd never learned why. Creator, rights, liberty, happiness. All such things were of the Fathers and not for us.

"How could you?" She asked.

Is it worth it? Adam's voice came to me.

"I want my life to be worth it," I told her.

Jona stood and shook her head. "I don't want this. I don't! And you don't either! From behind her back she pulled a little device I'd seen the admin use to talk to the uppers when she thought we weren't watching. "Did you hear?"

"Yes Jona, now do your duty."

"Five Hundred," Jona said, and lifted the box up over her head. She was going to bring it down on me, but I couldn't believe she would. My sister. My bunkmate and friend.

"No," I screamed, but she swung down, smashing it into the side of my head and lifting it again.

I collapsed as the blood flowed down my cheek. "For the Fathers" I heard Jona scream, but then, a loud crack split the air and she flew back from me.

The others lifted me with gentle hands, though each move felt like a bolt of fire ripping through me. As they carried me out into the open air, I saw Jona lying in a heap, unmoving.

Is it worth it?

They took me away from the tall glass building I'd lived in all my life, murmuring to themselves in a language I didn't know. The air tasted like smoke and the light of the sky burned into my eyes until I couldn't keep them open.

The woman who had screamed for Adam whispered next to my lolling head. "Your life for Adam's. Your life, your knowledge will save many like your friend before they have to die. And you will know what it is to have happiness before your life ends."

I smiled thinking about Adam.

I hoped he knew that what he'd done and what I would do would change things. That it all would be worth it.

FRAGILITY AND THE MODERN SISYPHUS

FRAGILITY

LUCY A. SNYDER

The worst offense that can befall
an upstanding white American
is neither death nor taxes, but an
accusation of racism.

You'd think it a truth universally
acknowledged, considering
the great wailing and gnashing
of so many middle-class teeth.

"I have Black and Mexican friends!"
they cry. Angrily, tearfully. Nobly
lining up unnamed acquaintances
in the thinnest of thin dark lines

. . .

To serve as unpaid human shields.
As if this is a game of Red Rover.
As if their neighbors' and coworkers'
obligatory friendly gestures were more

Than simple survival in this pale desert.
Smiling in the face of pain's a dictate
that a black or brown face dare not break
or they'll drown in an ocean of white tears.

As if it were a good character defense
to proudly claim to protect people
who are personally quite useful
but damn all the rest.

THE MODERN SISYPHUS

LUCY A. SNYDER

Your disbelief is a boulder
you blithely drop in my path:
Surely I am wrong
about what I've seen
with my own two eyes.
Surely I am sorely mistaken
about the brutalities many men
commit against most women.
Surely I exaggerate for effect.

I shove your rough skepticism
up yet another mud-slung hill
with well-supported statistics,
Pulitzer-grade investigative reports

and heart-wrenching memoirs.

The daily research is exhausting
but I push on, ever vainly praying
that facts might finally penetrate
your cheerful, willful ignorance
and you will stop treating me
as the unreliable narrator
of my own goddamned life.

VICIOUS

L. MARIE WOOD

S unlight and strawberries awaken the senses bright and new,
different every day.

Night comes to provide cover for discovering discoveries.

Many flavors, many scents, lessons learned and hours well spent.

Indelible, at least the parts that matter, delicious to the mind
and the senses,

nectar paired with condemnation and creation.

Some sweet like the drops of honey glaze,

some the assaulting kind, like black licorice on an unsuspecting
tongue.

Faded but not gone as the sun hides behind the clouds.

Ever there, if only as an echo, as rain obscures vision,

a phantom dancing on the periphery

ringing loud against a tin roof.

Raucous

shrill

all-consuming and selfish, if only in one's mind.

Blinding

invisible

pervasive.

Invasive.

Derisive.

Illusory.

Elusive.

Gone

gone

gone.

The haze of the veil,

Opaque and dense, streaked by resentful tears, indelible by weight, if not by sight, like a rider on weary shoulder.

Through shredded shears fearful eyes do watch as he comes,

forward

forward

always to

always due

whether paid with gold or blood

the man with the big hat and scraggly beard holds his marker true.

Quiet, quiet, slow the approach,

watches losses define wins and the former never top

As step after step, he still comes,

always true

goes he.

Tears blow in the wind to whet his whistle

what not syphoned to fill the bellies of those who'd bleed them dry.

And again.

And again.

And again.

Muted

slow

and oh, so dour rings the bell.

Come to it they must, through reluctance and despair,

trudging ever forward into the void,

leaving open their belongs and free their toil to walk into the abyss

the dark

the incorporeal.

Cosmic, the reach, cold, the touch.

Final, the grasp.

There.

There.

Ever.

Always.

FEEDING AMERICA

AUSTIN GRAGG

Trish propped her phone up against the glass tank on our kitchen table and started the latest video from her favorite news content creator. I'd finished setting up the terrarium last night, but my jars of dirt, moss, and twigs were still strewn about the counter around the small tank. I began tidying as she poured our coffee. Like every day, today's news was a doozy. On screen, a biosphere in another state, just like the one I worked at, was burning. I reached for her phone and lowered the volume. I'd rather not hear about it.

Every morning she turns on the news as if to say: please don't go, your facility could be next. Every morning I want to tell her: Don't send the kids to school, theirs could be next.

Different problems, she'd say. But the fear is the same. American. To live, she'd also say, we just have to live with it. The fear.

Mass shooters? Normal. But the people who'd bomb a biosphere —America's last bastions of agriculture—our country's entire food chain—either A) hated America, or B) "loved it" so much they didn't trust our government, or the vivariums feeding us— and wanted to either to legalize growing our own food again—

which Trish and I both thought was more than reasonable—or they wanted to rectify some harebrained conspiracy that the vivs were somehow violating human rights.

"Working with Michael still?" Trish asked in her low morning voice.

"Yeah. The newbie's a bit of a weirdo. He's probably itching for an attack on our building. Wouldn't be surprised if he's packing heat at work, horny at the thought of it."

"Sheesh. Another nationalist at the biosphere?"

I chuckled. "I don't know. He's hard to pin down. He's probably only rooting for himself. He's nice enough. Doesn't bring up politics. Which is fine by me. But yeah, they're definitely hiring new people with an eye on all that." I pointed to the protestors now on her phone screen. Some held signs decrying the new government supply chain, some with the faces of recently vanished activists, and others with the typical sentiments like: No Justice No Peace.

Trish handed me my coffee and I gulped the tart, burning black. Even after years of morning shift, I still wasn't used to being up so early. Usually, the smell and taste of coffee alone kicked me awake. But even the smell wasn't attractive. I held my breath as I sipped, and when the coffee hit my stomach, something wasn't right. It didn't settle to pressure my bowels to waking but roiled against the walls of my stomach and sent waves of nausea up my throat to swallow my head.

I rushed to the sink and let it come back up.

Trish rubbed my back. "You made a doctor's appointment, right?"

"I'll feel better before they can even see me," I said.

"You said that last time, too."

"So what layer is this?" Michael asked as he swept his light over the arched concrete ceiling, then traced the path until his light was useless against the dark.

"Drainage," I said. My nausea was gone, but Michael's voice was almost worse.

"Where's the water?" he asked. "I thought we'd be walking through a few feet of it when you showed me these waders. They feel a lot like my fly-fishing pants."

"Water's off, obviously. Which is why we have to work quickly. We can only divert so much of it for so long before it's a problem. We can't hold it in the reservoirs for long. Too old. Rust."

My new co-worker, Michael was at least twenty years my senior. Like so many others of his generation he'd reentered the workforce to stay afloat. Michael was also a moron. His explanations for so many things he simply didn't understand involved a capital T "They" and what *They* did or didn't want you knowing, or how *They* did or didn't want you behaving. I usually offered him Occam's Razor, but after seeing him refuse it so many times, if the blade were literal, I'd probably cut him with it. If it would shut him up. Especially down here.

"Oh, there's definitely something down here." Michael panted hard between words, clearly not used to climbing down the ladder in full gear.

There were plenty of stories about these old facilities, but of course the lower levels had the most. I didn't need his conspiracies or ghost stories. Drainage Level was spooky enough.

We stepped off the platform and our boots crunched atop the sea of rough, porous clay balls the size of my fist—hydro spheres, which filled the spillway. We were below the substrate and the vivarium itself, but above the artificial aquifer where water ran after filtering through the tunnels.

Michael aimed his flashlight down the long, pitch-dark corridor. Shadows leapt aside like his beam was a bullet train. Along the raised walkways shadows jittered in tandem with Michael's unsteady flashlight. Some of the shadows looked like heads, peeking out from behind the crumbling masonry. Peripheral shadows had provided decades of stories for the viv's workers.

I wiped mud from my work phone's screen protector and confirmed we were in the right spot on the map. The mile-marker denoted one of the hundreds of overflow drains—all of which were prone to occasional clogs. Michael crunched a few steps further into the dark as I cut my shovel into the rocky sea and began shoveling hydro spheres.

"All those stories," Michael said, voice echoing. "No other so-called haunted place has such a consistent record of people seeing the same things. Maybe the vivs really are hiding something?"

Michael sniffled, reminding me I should ask the doc at my appointment if vaccines were available again. I didn't need Mr. Anti-vax over there getting me sick and shortening my paycheck.

"You sound like a protestor," I said. "Careful or you'll vanish."

Michael laughed. "Whatcha think's down there?"

"If you make me dig this hole by myself," I said, "it'll be your body, 'cuz I'll put it there."

Michael scoffed but finally took the clue I needed a hand—and just in time for the five-minute warning tone to sound. Several garish red lights flashed along the spillway's path, both back toward the ladder, and further into the dark. The alarm stopped after five solid tones.

"It's just weird," Michael said, digging faster, "everyone sees those shadow people. The Fed denies anything's going on. For decades. What do you think?"

"I think..." I tossed the final scoop of clay and knelt to examine the blocked drain—a basketball sized hole with a rectilinear grate. "Maybe this is just a spooky-ass place—and people like telling stories about spooky-ass places—and our government doesn't owe anyone an investigation of spooky-ass little stories. No matter how long they've been told. Ever think of that, Michael? When you *do* think?"

"Jesus, man. Sorry. Was just talking."

I took a deep breath—one loud enough to express my regret for snapping at him. I popped off the grate and started scooping thick sludge from the drain. He finally, *finally* let some sweet silence pass between us. But of course, he was the one to break it.

"You okay?" he asked. "You've been quiet today."

I tightened my gloves and kept pulling out sludge. A pocket of either rot or still-forming methane hit my nose through my mask's filter, and I gagged. I'd barely made a dent in the clog. Damn it. This was going to take more than five minutes.

"I'm fine," I said. "Got a doctor's appointment today. Just nervous."

"Proctoscopy?" he asked, jest in his voice.

"No." I stood, rolled my aching shoulders, then pointed to indicate it was his turn to scoop slop. I wiped my hands on my waders. "I'll send in for another ten minutes." I opened my phone and poked at the map to extend the spillway pause.

"You feeling sick then?" Michael panted.

The app wasn't responding. I closed and relaunched it—and it stalled to load.

"No, Michael." The app loaded and I opened the map again. The menu with the option to pause sections of the spillway was blacked out and unresponsive to my pokes.

Then I saw it. Signal. We'd slipped off the Wi-Fi at some point. The phone was looking for a connection but couldn't grab one. I started back the way we came, clay spheres grinding under my feet.

"Lost signal," I said. "If I can't get it back, we need to jet as soon as the—"

The two-minute warning sounded.

"Damn it. Let's go."

"Hold on," Michael shouted over the tones. "It's almost clear."

"No," I said. "Don't play around with this."

"I've basically got it—"

"You'll basically be *dead* if you're not on the ladder when the water hits. Let's *go*."

"Shit! My boot's stuck!"

"Stuck?" I dropped my shovel and ran as fast as the rocks allowed.

Michael pulled hard on his left leg. It was buried in hydro spheres now. He leaned back against the wall of the small hole we'd dug, and it caved further in on itself. His breathing quickened as his leg stayed pinned below his knee.

"What is it?" I asked, clearing rocks as quickly as I could with my hands.

"Think something fell on my foot—under the rocks."

The alarm sounded. Not a dull tone, but a siren.

One minute.

I sprinted back for my shovel.

Michael screamed, like I was abandoning him. That gave me an unexpected stab in the ribs as my heaving lungs ached.

I came back and dug. Michael whimpered under the alarm. I wedged my shovel between his foot and the wall. Michael screamed and I worried I'd cut him. I levered the shovel until his leg drew free. We clawed our way out of the hole, filling it into a crater as we left and ran for the ladder. I knew I couldn't tell Trish about this as water roared distant, then deafening as we reached the ladder. Michael went first and I followed. The water swept furiously below us.

We stopped a few rungs up to attach our safety carabiners and Michael thanked me breathlessly. His flashlight was still on, clipped to his belt and swinging wildly above me.

"Kill your light," I said. "You're blinding me."

"Oh, sorry." He fumbled to grab his light, but didn't turn it off. He held the light on the tunnel wall behind us. I heard him curse under his breath. "What the hell is that?"

I looked. Something large clung to the brick wall and scurried on all fours into the dark.

"And why overtime *this* time?" Trish asked as she poured our morning coffee.

I stared at my terrarium, now full of microfauna, and wondered what to say. I didn't like the sound of a late-night shift to capstone a week of twelve-hour morning shifts. I'd be leaving again for work after dinner. But I said what I always do: Saying no is the chopping block. Career public servants are first up for cuts.

"We don't need it," she said. "We're not poor. Our debt is normal and—"

I thought about saying: "not for long, love." But I didn't. I watched a dairy cow isopod find the powdered food I'd sprinkled in the corner of the tank. How could I keep my composure? Should I, when talking about leaving and how soon? She hadn't asked about my appointment, but she also hadn't asked about the last one. We'd always been happy to assume we each had our own health under control. And why shouldn't we have? We had kids to focus on.

"Okay. Fine," she said. "But the boys are sleeping in our bed tonight. And I *swear*, if you won't hold and snuggle both me *and* our children *hard* this weekend—" she pointed at me and tongued her cheek. "—we'll riot. Philly. After a Superbowl."

I wanted to say: "If I quit now, I'll hold you every minute until I'm gone." But I wasn't ready to argue about me refusing treatment. They'd need every dollar of the overtime. Every day it could buy. I wasn't ready to explain how, for the kids, seeing me go through treatment, like their grandfathers did, and with a predetermined failure ahead... how it would traumatize them. About how it would cast a shadow over the way our children lived their own lives—with worries of diagnosis and death following them. Would they die like their father, and his father?

I backed away from the tank, its new life transforming it from terrarium to vivarium. How long would this little ecosystem live, if my family took care of it? Decades or more. Lifetimes even. Generations maybe. What fear ever existed in there—inside my little mimicry of nature?

"Riot like when they lose?" I asked.

"When they win."

"Damn." Sunlight cutting through the blinds striped her nose and sad smile in gold. I hugged her tight and she nestled into my neck. "I guess that means you'll get lots of snuggles when I get home."

M y appetite had increased sharply over the last week, but finding a moment in front of food while I wanted to eat was rare, so I ate quickly. Michael munched baby carrots like a deer while staring blankly past me. He was quiet this morning, but I had some pep in my step for the first time in days.

"You really think it was nothing?" Michael asked. "That thing."

"Shadow of the rapids under us," I said through bites. I'd thought about it more than I'd wanted to.

Before Michael could challenge the idea, a yellow alarm started. An alarm during lunch meant we wouldn't get a lunch. I wasn't sure Michael knew that. He put his sandwich down—I crammed the last part of mine into my mouth.

"You coming?" I asked. "Takes two to open the lungs." It took two to do almost anything in this place.

"What's this?" Michael nodded upward to the flashing lights and gentle tone as he followed.

"Air pressure. Incoming heat wave," I said.

I hadn't seen a heatwave in the forecast, but it wasn't rare to have sudden fluxes in the Midwest. The stale air in the lung chamber would be a problem for my nausea, but I'd fight it. Or maybe I'd tell Michael what was going on with me. Maybe telling him would get him to leave me alone. But at the same time I didn't want his pity. And the thought of telling Michael before Trish—no, just no.

"What's heat gotta do with the air pressure?" Michael asked as we closed our quarters behind us.

I started down the hall and waved for him to follow. "The vivariums are closed systems, remember?"

"Yeah." I'd be lying if, as my condition progressed, I said I didn't enjoy teaching Michael what I knew about the biosphere.

"Our evermore regular heat waves still affect the biosphere's temperature. Despite what some say, the Fed can't control climate. Heat means air expands."

"But the building is sealed tight so—" he was getting it.

"It has to have somewhere to go, or we risk damage to the building. So..." we reached the end of the long, white hall and I splayed my hands before the large steel door like a gameshow host, "we open the iron lung."

It took us a couple minutes of struggling with the door's locking wheel before it clunked open. We pulled hard to open the door. Inside, the iron lung's peeling white paint and rusted steel trim under the frail fluorescent lights made it look like an abandoned big box store. The true beauty, a masterwork of old-era engineering, hung above us—or rather, floated. The black dome ceiling was made of rubber and came together and down at its center to connect to the circumference of a steel disc, forty feet in diameter, hanging about twenty feet above us.

"What the hell is that?" Michael asked as I flipped on a few more lights.

The room was so large it could fit an entire block of matchbox houses like my own, maybe with their driveways, too.

"That," I said, "is the lung. The platform above us isn't held up by anything. The rubber ceiling isn't either. It's just differential air pressure. Neat, huh? Come here. Ever move two-thousand tons with one hand?"

I showed him how to grab one of the stabilizer feet hanging from the steel circle and shift the entire platform and ceiling with just his body weight. He snickered like a kid as everything over us lowered, and when he let go, floated back up and stilled.

"So, what do we do?" Michael asked.

"We're done," I said and pointed at the door we'd come through. "Opening the door opens the dampers. You'll only see this room when there's a heat wave."

"Is there a way into the vivarium from here?" Michael continued eyeing the room. "We'd be at ground level with it, right?"

"Over the drainage access path," I said. "But only inspectors go inside the viv."

"Were you ever an inspector?"

I laughed. "No. Haven't been here long enough to apply. Maybe one day."

"I thought ten years was enough to—"

A loud thud made us both jump. It came from beyond the doorway on the other side of the lung.

"What was that?" Michael asked.

"We're the only ones here, if that's what you're asking," I said. "Something probably fell over. Or…"

"Or?"

The flames from the news story this morning and on many other mornings came to mind. My heart raced. We had a responsibility to see what the sound was. It wasn't just our job—what our facility grew fed most of the state and tithed to the Fed. A fire would mean famine as governors politicked and the White House shrugged.

"Better make sure it was nothing," I said.

Michael didn't follow, but I wasn't about to make a newbie come with me. I'd been here two decades, since I was twenty-one. I'd applied because I believed in the biosphere's mission—cleaning up our country, feeding it good, healthy food. A mission missing its heart these years, but one I still wanted alive, nonetheless.

I held a hand up to Michael to say, *stay—I got this.* He nodded.

"I'll go get my phone," he said. "Just in case."

I crossed the long circular room quickly but slowed as I reached the double-wide open doorway. The hall beyond was an old maintenance corridor. Staff quarters used to be there when the viv was just a terrarium, but construction moved us my third year and closed off the old wing for storage.

"Hello?" I called. Were Michael's ghosts topside for a walk? If there were any ghost stories about the facility that took place above the lower levels, I hadn't heard any.

A shadow moved down the corridor. I gasped, then saw it was my reflection in a windowed door, distant and deformed at the end of the hall. But the door... the door was open.

I was frozen. Should I call someone? But what could happen in the time it took someone to respond? Trish. The kids. I wasn't here much longer, but would I throw precious time away to play hero? Was I self-righteous, a good little government employee, or just *right* to walk forward? I couldn't tell as I did. My legs took me without thought and I tensed, readying to spring into a conflict if I needed to. How had it all come to this? To a place where a two-person crew—or really just one, single civil servant could stand between six-million fellow Americans and a crisis.

"You're a liar," Michael said behind me.

What was obviously a gun barrel pressed into my spine. My heart stopped.

"I know you were an inspector," he said. "Take me into the vivarium."

We stood at the airlock between the maintenance sectors and the vivarium itself. My back was drenched in sweat. Was Michael a terrorist? He *knew* what hurting the viv would do to the state. I'd taught him everything I knew. Surely he understood the price was worth paying.

"We're only supposed to open it in an emergency," I said. I tried to keep my tone flat, like we were still working. "They'll know. They'll arrest us both or—"

"Or what? We'll work the fields?"

The hammer on the gun clicked and I started entering my emergency code on the keypad with slow, shaking fingers. Michael couldn't be a bomber. No. He'd just lost it. Postal. If he didn't kill me, what would he do to the vivarium? We'd starve the state and send who knew how many to die hungry—and for what? Justice?

"Faster," Michael said.

I took a deep breath as I pushed open the door and prayed to God Michael didn't blow me away over seeing the animals inside. We entered the pressure chamber. As the air shifted and our ears popped, I wondered if Trish had enough money to toll herself and the kids into another state. I wondered if they had enough food to last through the panic buying until the dispersal of the reserves. If they stayed.

How would she tell the kids? How *could* she? Would they ever know it all? Should they? Should anyone?

The door opened to the green. A picture like Eden in a children's Bible. Greener and more alive than any garden I'd ever seen. Blooms spotted the beds lining the path forward. Pollinators roamed. I let the grassy air fill me.

Michael sobbed and shuddered as he walked out into the field before us. I followed to the crest of the hill, overlooking the sea of crops. Through Michael's jacket, I could see the bulky shape of whatever he must have strapped to his chest when he went back to our quarters. Thick boxes up and down his back and sides.

When he saw the laborers, he screamed. And I recognized it. The same scream from the drainage level, when he'd thought I was about to leave him for dead. I wish I'd screamed like that when I first saw them. But I'd been so sure the price was just.

In Michael's scream, for the first time, I was unsure.

They came to us. Naked over the hills. The newly sentenced still walked on two legs and carried shovels and tools like the ones I'd been issued, eyes wide at the sight of us. Others, born inside, crawled on all fours, blackened by the soil, wearing foliage in their hair, toothless mouths wide as they shrieked and keened and darted for us.

Michael dropped to his knees.

Before I could think a selfish, fearful thought, I closed the door behind us.

THE TRAVELING FREAK SHOW

LINDSEY BETH GODDARD

The traveling Freak Show arrived in town;
The strutting of hooves and stirring of dust
Were unnerving to Hope, who battled a frown
At the sight of those cages, all covered in rust.

The afternoon crowd, in their fancy attire,
Had paraded like ants into the square,
And while the Ringmaster had the look of a liar
He offered wonders, which in these parts were rare.

Hope was a young man; Hope had a curse,
An empath who'd never found his purpose.
As each carriage parked, his plight grew worse,
For something was amiss with this circus.

. . .

Pockets fat with ticket stubs and cash,
    The Ringmaster announced the first freak.
Then, he pulled back the curtain in a flash
Smiling as the audience gasped and shrieked.

Justice sat chained, dead-center in her cage,
    Her pretty face devoid of any eyes.
The weight of her scales, too heavy to gauge,
Caused her weakened arms to droop at her sides.

Another curtain loomed, as black as a wraith.
    "And now for something truly pathetic!"
He drew back the drape, unveiling Faith,
Chest open, her sacred heart prosthetic.

Hope wanted to leave, to turn and escape.
    He whimpered as the eager crowd cheered.
A sheer affront to his heart was taking shape,
But to flee would mark Hope a traitor here.

He shuddered as a third curtain was pulled,
    To reveal the prone form of Liberty,

And how the crowd's sick curiosity was fueled

By that shackled freak in cage number three.

H er rainbow skin had dulled to muted tones,

Barely showing her true, brilliant pigment.

Still, Liberty glowed, though skin and bone,

Like she knew pain but longed to transcend it.

H ope drew nearer. In fact, Hope got too near.

(The Freak Show had been seeking one more.)

The Ringmaster nabbed Hope before he could disappear,

Trapping him in cage number four.

T he man saw in Hope a true oddity,

For in his Hope's eyes of blue, brown, and green

Swirled a patient love for all humanity,

A rare trait, unheard of… unseen.

T he Ringmaster planned for the newest freak

To be tortured by a crowd's daunting jeers

Until that poor boy, so tender and unique,

Had filled many buckets with his tears.

. . .

So, on rolled the freaks, onto the next place,
 Hope in the cage that trailed Liberty,
And through the bars, she gazed at Hope's face,
Until those eyes were all she could see.

Words can't explain the deep love found that day,
 How Hope ignited Liberty's lost light.
Her colors grew brighter, and a sudden blaze
Rendered those chains dust that once bound her tight.

The Freak Show arrived with two cages empty
 At the next stop. The crowd stirred, unimpressed.
And though Hope and Liberty had both gone free,
They'd soon be back for Faith and Justice.

THE FIRST LAW, UNBENDABLE UNTIL SNAPPED

ANTON CANCRE

We say we say we should be able to say
whatever it is that we want to say
We say we say that such things are our
God-given rights as citizens and kings
when we want to talk about bathrooms
and sports teams and hormones and biology
or crime rates and invisible sand-drawn
lines that can never be crossed,
from the one side, at least, if not from this one
or when it is appropriate to discuss death
and, more pointedly, its causes at the end
of forty five copper jacketed slugs per second
and especially when we want to scream out
the simultaneous all powerful powerless THEY

that are trying to breed us out of existence

And we say we say it is all just expression

and we say we say that all expression is just

while sewing lips shut and burning hands

to stumps; smashing, cutting, slashing down

when words don't match the pre-approved lists

we have painstakingly posted in five point font

in the sub-basement room, fifth door to the right,

of the county affairs office with no first floor entrance

behind a sign warning of underfed grizzly bears.

In the sole-sacred name of Jesus. Ahmen.

PURSUIT OF HAPPINESS

CAPITALISM KISSES YOUR SELF-CARE COMMODIFIED SMILE INTO CASH

TK BRAVE

<($)> <($)>

Dear darling citizen-victim of my end stage empire
I am your sex-sells siren dollar sign tease
crooning corporate shame-serenade melodies

For the bargain low price of your civil rights advocacy and self-esteem
only my luxury Laissez-faire cream is capable of
concealing your imperfect complexion and deep-seated skin of insecurities

So open your greed, turn from charitable to heritable wallet
pledge allegiance to my brand name products

and my fingers will creep, stroke your billfold deep and so sweet

B udgets are moral documents and you are debt's embodiment

incorrectly conflating corporate success and shallow wanton compliments

with self-care, emotional connection, and authentic confidence

S plurge on my Happiness Industrial Complex planned-obsolescence pleasure

fill your empty shopping cart of a broken heart with my mass-market kitsch

press infinite cash kisses to my fiscal lips to immortalize your once iconoclastic

smile   plastic
        into a   card
            stiff   credit
                vapid grin of

COUNTING SHEEP

KEN HUELER

Fast, immediate, hard, I slam into one of the trees. No pain. I palm my face. No blood, but the topology's both right and wrong—from being in a dream, or from the CPAP mask? Everywhere, the whisper-shush of a small fan. I'm at the threshold of a large perfect circle of tall grass surrounded by woods. No saplings, no fallen ancients, just towering trees with ascending fungal disks and exhausted black and yellow leaves. Every branch, each leaf I touch feels dusted with granules of dried sap.

I spin into the open space, laughing. I've never lucid dreamed in my life. Is this what normal sleep feels like?

From across the glade, a man squeezes between two trees: He's taller than me, thinner than me, better dressed than me. Why aren't I dressed better? No one should be shabby in their own dream. An orange octopus hides the stranger's face. Suckered arms grip shoulders, squeeze the neck, push red hair into tufts. Only the man's eyes are visible.

I ask, What are you supposed to be?

The octopus slides up, disappearing the man's eyes and unveiling his mouth. "Tell me, Foster: What is a dream?"

This, of course.

"This?"

Yes, this.

The figure advances uncertainly through the tall, amber-colored grass, toward my voice. "Dreams come in two varieties: unaware and aware. This"—grand gesture—"is your subconscious sorting the day's information, acting out your fears and joys, playing. So, tell me: What am I supposed to be? What does this overblown fairy circle mean? Why an octopus? Odd, to build this kind of dream, Foster. Odd, odd, odd. You don't know, do you?"

I bristle. The other kind of dream is aspirational, isn't it? Well, isn't it?

"Yes. A conscious choice, a concrete goal with steps—plausible or not." A hand on my shoulder, a rubbery orange arm exploring my neck. "Why are your aspirational ones always petty and dull, so predictably disappointing?"

I jerk back and stare at the only available eyes: those wide-set horizontal black slots in bulging, speckled circles. Leave me alone.

He splays all ten fingers against his sternum. "Aren't you already, trapped in this skull with only yourself for company?"

I snort and retreat back into the trees. Soon they unravel into a manicured clearing, larger than the first, with gardens and a fussy thatched cottage, all wrapped in a white picket fence. I scan for a road or a path. Not one break in the perfect circle of trees and shrubs. Why? Is my brain embodying social isolation? The thought burns like an honest, accurate insult.

Crying, outright wailing, pours from the cottage. I stagger forward, as if stepping onto an abruptly tilting hill. I accelerate across the grass and through an open gate until a rustic plank door stops me dead. Again, no damage or pain.

Are you all right in there?

The screaming rises. I pound on the door, yell. Nothing. I grip the doorknob—sticky, like the trees—and push into a single room with a king-sized bed, a spinning wheel, a writing desk, a wide wooden table, and a crib. My eyes lock onto a woman cradling a howling, ugly, bruised baby. For a moment, I can't speak.

What happened?

She glances to its face—scarlet, purple, blue—and back, defiant.

Inside my skull the wailing expands, impossibly loud. A shriek whittles into a single, enduring, high-pitched scream that creaks against the bones in my head.

Can't you shut that damn kid up?

She sets the baby into the crib. "As if strangers can tell us how to raise our own children. If you think it's that easy, get one of your own and have a go." She strides to a window, opens it.

I rush over, spin her around, grab her shoulders. Her collar bones dig into my palms. Then, mortified by my assault, I let go and jump back.

"Oh," she mutters, "it's that kind of dream, then?" She reaches behind her neck. The dress falls.

Electricity fires through my torso. The baby must be just as loud, but its cries melt to muffled, underwater echoes.

She sinks onto her pooled dress. "Let's pretend you're my husband, coming home, and you have absolute spousal rights."

She slaps her palms on the floor and leans forward. "That means anything is possible. Anything."

I'm frozen. I need to leave/I want to stay. She has a ring. Is the man from the other clearing her husband?

Behind her, Octopus Face crawls through the open window, flops inside and stands. The octopus drifts around his head, revealing then hiding patches of red, sucker-scored skin. "Intoxicating, isn't it, this kind of power?" The woman rises, and he wraps an arm around her waist, looks upon her face.

"Weakness and obedience combine into one hell of a drug."

She smiles.

"Do you like my home? My wife? Human history is ownership, followed by pointless uprisings and reshuffling, and then, always, back to ownership. Thus…" He waits, his breathing a continuous whirring whisper.

I can't think of anything to say.

He releases the woman, who darts to her dress, and he approaches the crib. "Our modern American dreamers—the robber barons and the Puritans—are marrying, and if their dream comes true, we'd better be one of their children." He lifts the baby, inserts a candy pacifier—so very red—cherry?—into its mouth. The screaming stops, leaving only slower tears and pacing eyes. The man sighs, returns the child to the crib. "A compliant child, that is. One who accepts the dream offered. Do you agree?" He waits. "You're letting me down, Foster. Your job, your role, your reason for existence is to elevate yourself in the Outside. And you haven't. Do you know how galling it is for me, a creature of dreams, to be trapped in a poor man's head?"

I'm not poor.

"Always afraid of losing your job, your house, your health. That is poor. And your pathetic dread," the octopus colors red, glares; the man kicks the crib, "it permeates my world with a sticky invisible film. Why continue to be dull even here, Foster? All this is you. You can order into existence a palace, summon servants, concubines, and slaves. Owning all that sounds good, doesn't it? The certainty, the power. But Here it won't be real. Instead, you are called on to do all that in the Outside. I will guide you. Listen to instinct, gut feelings, those tiny nags in the back of your skull, for that is my voice."

I edge toward the door. At a gesture, his wife runs, arrives first. She leans against the frame, splays her arms, shakes with terror.

"Where would you go?" he roars. "One cannot escape without a border, and a dream world has no edge."

I run to the open window. As I vault out, something trails along my calf.

His voice—close, immediate: "What are you doing?"

I don't know. I bolt for the woods. Above the trees, I glimpse buildings, veer that way.

"You don't need to! Just get back here and do what I tell you." His voice farther, not chasing: "Without me, you're homeless—I can tear down anything you build; without me, you're defenseless—I'll make you suffer; without me, you are alone—for in Here, only I am real."

The trees in this area are wider apart and easy to thread. I can almost run—but where? I need an exit. For that, I need information. To get that, I need help.

I stop at a cluster of trees. He said everything here is me, told me I could summon things. Each of you contains a spirit. Come out to me. Figures—humanoid, amber yellow, startled—obey, oozing through bark and fungus. Show me the exit.

One steps forward. "You created us. How would we know what you do not?"

You're a part of my mind.

Another presses a finger to my forehead: "You are the logical one. Tell us"

Frustrated, disgusted, I storm away. Those damned creatures follow and more keep emerging. I speed up to stay ahead of them. And of Octopus Face. Then, directly in front of me, he explodes from a tree.

"You'll never leave this forest unless I let you," he yells. I jog left. "Just wander, wander, wander, along with your little children."

I round on him. No. I can't sleep forever.

"Forever? No one can. But for the remainder of your life? A coma, Foster. You need wakefulness to control your mind, but I do not." The octopus arches two arms, rips the man's scalp into flaps and tears out a wide plate of skull. "Within this warm bubble of bone, I could rule our shared brain until you die, form and wipe away planets, birth giants, do whatever I please." He bows. Inside his skull, planets and stars bubble into existence then explode; faceless albino giants stride across a vast lawn of naked fleeing humans; the man and his wife hover over their table, dissecting my chained body. Octopus Face retrieves his shard of skull and turns it several ways until, like puzzle piece, it clicks into place. He smoothes his scalp flat, and the octopus scrambles up. "So, you see, you are expendable. Act like it."

You'd torture me?

"If you kept me from what I want, of course." He lurches forward. "But I'd rather not. Inducing a coma—with a distraction or whispering you into a bad decision or impulse— would be a risk to us both." He wipes his hand across a bush, drags his fingers down my face. "Your brain is sticky and dull. Imagine the pig sty you'd create without external stimulation. Give me a better world, Foster, and I won't take away yours." He scans. "My goodness, how many of these damned people are you going to make?"

The crowd is almost a wall. Red splotches are blooming across their skin. I didn't want this.

He laughs. "Lying to your subconscious? Remember, I am the quiet part who, deep down, really gets you. Only one—one!— was required for information, but you needed a mob, didn't you? That's natural and normal—we all want the many. A multitude of bodies is the gateway to paradise: The survival instinct enslaves the chosen while the rest starve as warnings." He cocks his head. "Sound familiar?"

I shoulder through the crowd.

"Wouldn't you," he yells, "rather do the chasing?"

I've got two options: Find an exit—although there might not be one—or run out the clock. When my eyelids open, I'm free. But either way I'll be dragged back here for the rest of my life. How do I seize control? Sleep specialists treat nightmares, but I only get one free session, and with my lousy insurance I can't—

Stay back, I tell the figures, now closing in on the sides and cutting ahead of me. Their red blotches have suffused through their yellow skin, tinging them orange. More appear ahead. I warned you to stay back! I yell, punching hard into a face. Soft, sticky—like a plushie doll mottled with dried jam.

Don't make me hurt you. They fall back. This feels good, taking control, but they still follow. Go back inside your trees. None retreat.

Because I'm thinking about them, they exist. Octopus Face—except for that first meeting in the glade, every time he's crossed my mind he's shown up.

Don't think about pandas! I yell. My mother used to say that, just randomly, for fun. And of course I would think about pandas—how couldn't I? Don't think about pandas, I chant, skipping now. Laughing.

And I'm out!

The sky is still bright and blue, but the sun is missing. A road runs perpendicular to me. Across it is a bamboo forest. I step onto the asphalt. One direction leads to an ocean, the other to a city. Behind me the figures wait at the threshold of forest. Leave me alone, I bark.

My stupid brain's a wreck from months of stress and insomnia. I focus on my breathing, on the constant pulsing fan of the CPAP machine. I tap into my body, lying in the sleep clinic's safety bed. I feel me.

I check on the figures, now fading back into yellow. They've raised their arms; their toes are rooting into the soil.

I choose the city, shoes loud as they pull against the tacky asphalt. Some niggle in my brain tells me this direction is good, but does that come from me or Octopus Face? Hunches are his voice.

Laughter. "Don't think about pandas!"

I've thought about him! I break into a run. The city must be miles ahead, but I won't tire. There, I'll have more places to hide; I can see where I'm going and see him coming; buildings are less complicated than trees, so imagining things onto or into them must be easier. I start early, picturing wide, grid-patterned streets feathered with car-excluding bollards. That will be my city.

I need to go faster. Lucid dreamers—they can fly. I raise my arms. Nothing. I hop, drift down like a lunar explorer. Clawing the air does nothing. I close my eyes, focus. Just the sounds of the omnipresent fan and my shoes peeling off the tacky road.

The film.

I focus on that, my feet. Leaning forward, almost falling, I sprint. The extra traction propels me forward. Just feet and road and mind.

The road is ruler straight, but I stumble startled into the city as if rounding a corner. Behind me are buildings I didn't pass. Ahead, I hear shouts and screams. Not one person in sight.

The hell I'd imagine this, I mutter, but the streets are indeed wide and blocked off and square. I seek the taller buildings—that seems right. But isn't this all just hide-and-seek? And what if there's no portal? Waking. Is there a way to force that?

Yes, I realize, yes, there is.

I zig-zag the blocks. Buildings scatter, deflect, and amplify the din of terrified people. I reach what must be the financial district —a spite fence of dick-measuring skyscrapers—and run up a hotel's half-circle passenger drop-off. Past revolving doors and an empty lobby I locate two facing banks of elevators, three to a side, and slam the call button. A chime. I rush in. The top floor requires tapping a room key, so I punch the one under. I stare into the vast lobby: An arm or a foot or the press of a button could stop the doors at any second.

Slam. Jerk. Rise.

I made it!

All the panel's disks, except the top floor's, light up.

Second floor. The doors slide and I jackhammer the close button. Same with the third floor and the fourth. Panic returns:

I've trapped myself in a tiny metal box, a double-wide coffin, really. What if it stops between floors? Or Octopus Face steps through the doors?

Fifth. I need a second way out. I look up: a ceiling hatch. By law, only a rescue crew can unbolt it.

Sixth. But do laws matter in my own dream? I'll write my own. As the doors shut, I jump, punch the hatch. Solid.

Seventh. Something large drops down. "Whence all this spunk, Foster? And why directed at me, not on conquering the There?"

I push free, shove myself out the opening elevator. Each hallway door I try is locked. "You don't exist," I shout. "Neither of us do. Not here."

He rapidly taps the elevator panel, leaning to watch me. "Why fight? Each time you sleep, we'll meet."

The doors shut. I run, hit the call button. All the elevators except the one I was riding rise from the lobby. Floor two, then three—not stopping—six, seven. Five elevators open. I glance up—Octopus Face is paused on nine. I rush into one and press twelve. Thankfully, only that one button lights.

Nine.

Ten. Will I pass him? How much head start might I have?

Eleven.

Twelve. Another hallway of numbered doors. I rush left, turn right, see an emergency fire stairway. I hit the door with my shoulder and the crash bar with my hip. One flight up, no more stairs, just a propped-open door. Through it, on the facing wall, is a sign with arrows and room numbers, and a second that says 'Ice' and 'Pool'. I barrel that way.

Sunlight. A windowed door. The handle yanks from my hand. A desperate man shoulders me aside and runs toward the emergency stairwell, and an almost physical punch of sound hits me: All the city's screaming, shouting, crying, and laughing is here, but five times louder. A crowd—Christ, how many?—fills the patio. I can't tell how far the roof goes. I spot an open space and shove my way over. A swimming pool. People jostle neighbors in, and those inside clamber and tread others underwater. The orange octopus bubbles to the surface. Human fingers wrap around a chrome hook ladder.

Move it! I shout at everyone. Get out of my way. I beat on the woman ahead of me—Stupid bitch, I said 'move'—until hands and arms and then bodies crush me into her. That man in the hall, he was fleeing—to the ocean, the bamboo forest, the woods, the cottage? Why? I'm trapped now, only one choice left.

"Imagine ordering them to part…and they do! The power! And those who don't obey, well, everyone is free, free to choose starvation, jail, cancer-rot, suicide. Remember, Foster, there is no American Dream: There are many. So very many. Choose big, choose long, and either take that—by force if necessary—or live on scraps and cast-offs."

The woman I'm plastered to pitches forward. The crowd forces me after her, down, into one of many human cascades pouring off buildings—a falling, screaming, terrified tumble of shoes and flailing limbs and shopping bags and urine. I could hear them earlier, why didn't I see them?

"What dream does a quitter get? None, or someone else's. I can save you, Foster, but only if we unite in the same dream."

I turn. He's clawing through jumpers, closing the distance. I kick the man beside me, launching myself down, grab a ponytail and pull. I swim body to body, clawing shirts, legs, hair.

"In the coming uprisings, assassinations, and unrest, leaders must emerge. Either men fight for our favor and women kneel before us, or we become the latest version of slaves." A tug on my arm. "Join me, Foster."

Launching a heel into his armpit, I float free, grab and fling a child. He knocks it aside, but it slows him. A teen I'm using as a rung swings a fist into my ribs, sending me into a woman's wild, kicking legs. I veer against somebody who elbows me. These painless blows make my course more erratic, widen the distance between me and Octopus Face. I lean into it, put cruelty into my actions.

I catch glimpses of thick red mist. I've heard that falling dreamers wake up just before hitting the ground, but what if I can't see it? I'd fall forever, down, down, down until morning.

An old man bites my leg. No pain, just blinding frustration and an available nose to vent it on. He reels left, and I get it, the answer: sideways. To see the pavement, asphalt, whatever, I need to go out, away from the others. I tear through the compacting crowd, pass the old man. Someone I inconvenience kicks the small of my back in the luckiest way.

And I am free! How is the street still so far away? Without bodies around me, I have nothing to change my trajectory, but I'm far enough out to see the ground. I dive, head down, arms out, eyes glued to a space between two bollards, which seems about where I'll land.

Something wet, soft, and solid hits back of my head.

Hissing whispers. Pressure on my skull, creeping around my upper arms, my neck. A suckered arm's tan underside whips into view, slams against my mouth. I don't need to breathe, so I reach my right hand to my opposite shoulder. The orange arm, tinging red, is like a plush toy—velvety, smooth, mushy—but laced with powerful muscles. I'm bigger, though, and suckers don't stick to cloth. My left hand yanks my right arm free.

Struggling, something flips me over, and I spot the man, out from the crowd and unable to catch up. I twist, so as not to miss seeing the impact. The octopus creeps across my head. I reach up with both hands, seek its eyes. Liquid runs down my forehead though I have not broken its skin. Am I bleeding? I didn't feel a beak chew into my scalp. But it's black, it's ink. Trying to blind me with ink. I reposition my head to protect my eyes. More arms swing to my face, roil, lace like fingers, converge into slow, drooping eyelids. I pull and twist to keep my sight clear.

There: From one partially blocked eye I see asphalt. The octopus skids down my forehead. Screaming, I reach behind the thing's head and tear the monster off. Pain, pressure—two men gripping my arms, another kneeling on the mattress, palms on my sternum.

"Foster! Foster, it's okay. You're awake now."

The CPAP mask teeters in front of me, off, but still attached by the lower neck strap. I quit fighting. Cautiously, the three nurses let go. I try to sit, but the bed's waist belt limits me to propped on elbows. This sleep therapy room—not the same. Larger.

A fourth man, a tall redhead behind banks of machines, is removing an elaborate headset. "You woke early, Foster." He peels EEG disks from his head.

"What did you find out?"

He waves dismissively. "A sleep therapist will read your data and contact you."

One of the nurses is detaching the EEG disks I didn't yank off. Another smiles. "Would you like some juice? Coffee?"

I peer around him. "Then who are you?"

He walks to the bed. "I'm from the experiment side, the one paying your compensation and free sleep therapy."

"And?"

"Good, good! Generally, as predictably disappointing as most, but you also exhibit a stubborn rebellion we're hoping to weed out. That makes you... useful to us."

"Wait, what?" As I grab for the CPAP's still-attached neck strap, my knuckles brush stubble—several day's worth. "I came here yesterday. No, not here—where am I? And for how long?" I run a hand through my hair. Pain. I walk my fingers back, to a shaved circle around taped gauze and what feels like a cable.

A nurse notices. "Don't play with that. You injured your head."

I fumble with the waist restraint, seeking the buckle. "Against what? It's a goddamned safety bed."

The nurses converge on me. I push backward with my arms and backpedal my heels. Hands drag me back, knees push me flat.

"You need to be fully wake. We don't want you hurting yourself again."

"Let me out! I have rights."

One of the nurses strokes my cheek. "Relax. You had a nightmare, that's all."

The redhead slides his face down to mine, creases and circles from the elaborate headset still livid in his skin. "Improved sleep and a little money—wasn't that the dull, petty dream you chose? And here it is, realized! You'll sleep more than ever before, Foster. Oh, and do you have a favorite charity?" He nods at the nurses. "Prep him for another session."

. . .

A mask is pushed against my face—not the CPAP: this has a faint, sweet smell. The man joins the nurses in restraining me.

"Ready for that coma we talked about?"

FAKE MUSE

ANGELA YURIKO SMITH

*G*ive me your tired, your poor, your huddled masses yearning
to breathe free.

"Bullshit." Glenda huffed. Her great-grandmother had been one
of those huddled masses. She had left everything behind hoping
to build a future for her children. Her grandmother had never
been able to rise from the huddled mass. She came from a place
where the sea caressed the abundant and fertile land. She gave
that up for America where everything had a cost. She came for
the dream and stayed for the nightmare.

The guard that had checked Glenda's ferry stub glanced over at
her small outburst and she lowered her eyes. That had been
stupid. She was white-passing until someone asked for her
papers. She was almost free of this land. She had been awarded
her passport. All she had to do was make it to John F. Kennedy
by 11 tonight and she should be on her way, like her great-
grandmother, to build a new life. She cradled her belly with one
hand and corrected herself. *Lives.*

Mother of Exiles…

Now we are all exiles, she thought. Her great-grandmother had left a place where fruit grew on trees, where you could be hungry but never starve. Glenda had never eaten a fruit, though she often thought about them. The stories had passed from her great-grandmother to her grandmother. Fruit was heavy, sweet and full of syrup. Glenda had been dreaming about fruit for the last month. Her mouth watered. She took a sip of her Patriot Tea and tried to imagine the taste of Apple.

Coming here was an impulse, but it felt so necessary. It was like saying goodbye for her family. They had only been on this soil four generations, but Glenda could never just ghost a one night stand like her friends. Maybe that's how the baby in her belly had defied her No Bearing status. This baby did not respect the Bad Genetics ban. This baby was a rebel. Glenda wanted this baby more than fruit.

Glenda knew she should just go to the airport. There was no room in this world for sentiment. Her great-grandmother had been sold a lie. Now Glenda had a chance to go to another place and start a new life. She hoped she had chosen better. She patted her chest where the ticket and her Passthrough was hidden, taped to her skin beneath her bra strap. She looked up to see the guard watching her. Too fast, too guilty, she averted her eyes. She could feel his interest on her like a conviction. She needed to go. She tried to focus back on the plaque, feigning interest.

Y*our huddled masses yearning to breathe free,*
The wretched refuse of your teeming shore.
Send these, the homeless, tempest-tost to me…

. . .

Glenda whispered the words, like a prayer, to demonstrate her focus. She felt the guard moving. The few people in the museum moved away like oil on water. She heard the heavy glass doors open and footsteps shuffle quickly through. It was just after noon, but suddenly it felt late to her. Suddenly John F. Kennedy, just under two hours away by subway, felt like an impossible journey. It felt like the pressure in the room had dropped, like she was underwater.

"Ma'am…" His voice came from too close and she flinched.

"Yes?" She turned to him with a carefully practiced casualness. "Sorry, you startled me. I was so engrossed in our Great History, the Greatest Ever."

He studied her. She tried not to look him in the eye, but she could already see how he was looking at her. That look either meant she was in for pain or his pleasure. If she played along she might get it over with in time to leave, then no more time for sentimentality. It would be straight to the airport for her.

"What's your name?"

He had a little bit of an accent. Maybe somewhere in the midwest. It had soft edges.

"Glenda. Like the Good Witch." She smiled at him, at the human she hoped he would be.

He studied her. "What do you have in your shirt?"

She hadn't expected that. "Nothing. I mean, my Passthrough. I keep it there in case I get robbed."

He sucked up his bottom lip, glanced to the left and then held out his hand. "I need to see it please."

Glenda could feel hope falling out of the air like cold mist, dampening her spirits. She shivered. "Yes sir."

Her mind raced. If only she hadn't put them together in the same envelope. If only she hadn't given it away with a nervous pat. If only she hadn't come here at all. She slid her hand into her shirt and tugged the oft-recycled envelope free. Her skin stung where the tape pulled free. Slowly, she slid the envelope out from her blouse and placed it on his waiting palm.

He opened the envelope without removing the contents. He pulled out her Passthrough, without removing the plane ticket. He sifted through the pages, looking at the approval stamps. He got to the page with her photo and name. He studied the page, then her.

"You don't look like a Nguyen."

She cleared her throat. This conversation. "It's my father's name."

"What's it? Asian? You don't look Asian. You adopted?"

"My mother was white." No one was left in the Museum.

He pried the envelope open and read her ticket without removing it then replaced her Passthrough before handing the precious packet back to her. Cautiously, she took it back, her hand trembling. She was struck without words, her stomach threatening to shatter and let her collapse. She held on.

"Thank you…" Maybe he hadn't seen the ticket. She had bought it legally. It was for an approved trip. Only she knew she intended it to be one way. She had told no one her intention. Maybe this day she had been lucky.

"You should get going while you can," he murmured. It was soft enough she almost couldn't understand him. Then, louder. "Looks like you have everything in place. You need to move on and stop wasting my time."

"Yes… yes!" Glenda could barely breathe. "Sorry, sir. I will leave you alone." She stuffed the ticket back beneath her bra strap, hastily pressing it into place with some of the remaining tape and stumbled to the side. "I'll go now… thank you."

She risked a glance at his face and then away. His expression was hard to read, but Glenda could risk no more. Grateful to this stranger, she hurried out of the museum, only pausing to drop her remaining drink in an empty bin as she passed. Then it was straight to the dock where she boarded the ferry to Battery Park as soon as they opened boarding.

From there, she had her directions. She had memorized them as a song so she wouldn't need to write them down. She had sung it as a lullaby to the secret life she was smuggling within her. She found a seat off to the side on the deck and folded into it as discreetly as possible. Under her breath, she hummed her directions to herself, softly and barely audible.

W alk to Bowling Green station and take the 5 subway line to Fulton Street.

Transfer to the A train and then ride to Howard Beach.

Then take the AirTrain to Terminal C.

By this time tomorrow we will be free!

S he looked back at Liberty Island as the ferry gently pulled away, leaving the so-called Mother of Exiles behind. She was a false goddess, just more fake muse. *Perhaps that isn't her fault,* thought Glenda. *Perhaps that is the role she has been forced into, like so many of us. Isn't she, herself, an immigrant?*

The air was thick with salt and sorrow. The only other time she had visited this place was with her grandmother, the first generation of her family to grow up in this new land. Things had been so different then. Her grandmother excitedly told the much younger Glenda about all the opportunities she must grow up to inherit. Grandma's broken English was more accepted then and not something to be detained over. She had, however, been detained even then. Even in the Golden Age of the nation there had always been the same dangers for anyone with roots too close to the surface and still visible.

This trip, alone and with her next generation secreted within her womb, was different. There were no excited grandmothers here now, telling stories of hope for the future. There was hardly anyone at all. As a child she remembered having to sit in her grandmother's lap because there were more people than seats. This trip, there was a small handful, gathered in silent ones and twos. No one shouted and paid homage to this national icon.

T he ferry guard was making his rounds, looking directly at each passenger, reporting. There was always reporting now, everyone after a little bit of the Alien Ejection Fund. Find an illegal, get paid. The problem was, everyone who touched that illegal got a tiny slice from the initial reporter to the detention center that awaited them at the end, so it was in everyone's best interest to ignore the truth. Deport and get paid.

If her last name didn't make her a target, Glenda might even turn in a few people herself. As it was, it was only a matter of time for her. Her own mother had vanished shortly after the New Republic took power. At the time, everyone said she had abandoned her daughter. Glenda had been angry with her mother for years. Later, she wondered if her mother had abandoned her, or been apprehended early, when AEF was only known to a very few.

Conspiracists whispered that the dearly deported were sold for the only thing they had left of value—body parts. Livers, lungs and the like, stored like shoes for richer people to come shop for, so the whispers said. It probably wasn't true, but no one had ever heard from a deportee to refute the rumor, so it thrived. Glenda turned her gaze away from the horizon and focused on the mechanical rumble beneath her feet. Above, gulls circled languidly, indifferent to the panicked fluttering of her heart.

The guard strolled past her part of the deck, mumbling low into his radio. She pretended not to notice him and feigned exhaustion, an easy enough thing to do. Nearly everyone was exhausted these days, two and three jobs needed just to eat. Luckily, he paused, studying her, but then passed on. She let herself exhale and then took in a deep breath. Air, at least, was still free

Her fingers instinctively pressed against the small envelope taped close to her skin, reassuring herself it was still there, still secure. Across the water, Manhattan approached slowly, its skyline defined prominently by One World Trade Center, a striking silhouette rising defiantly into the sky. This gleaming symbol had risen from the ashes of tragedy, created as a testament to resilience and renewal. Both resilience and renewal were needed and, like everything else, in short supply.

The breeze tousled her hair, almost tenderly, but it did little to soothe her nerves. A few of her fellow passengers had stood up and gathered near the exit, careful to avoid eye contact with each other—each lost in their personal dramas. What was once an uneventful ferry ride, a child's transition between sightseeing and lunch, now felt like an act of subversion.

Approaching the dock, she was surprised to see the state of the Battery Maritime Building with only one of the original three grand arches still functioning as a ferry slip. The arches, once adorned with ornate iron and copper work, were now stripped. Separated by pilasters, the cupolas that crowned the turrets were now shrouded in tattered plastic sheets that snapped in the afternoon breeze. The building's facade, once a rich palette of colors and intricate detailing, had now been robbed and repurposed to decorate homes of the privileged.

Nothing expressed patriotism these days like remodeling with authentic vintage history. Glenda closed her eyes and tried to remember the building as she had first seen it, bright, noble and grand. How excited her grandmother had been to show it to her, rattling off facts in her Pidgin English.

The briny scent of the harbor, mingling with the distant aromas of the few street food vendors that still lined the park brought her back. Seagulls called overhead, their cries blending with the sounds of the ferry docking with a gentle thud as the vessel met the pier. The vibrations resonated beneath her feet, itchy to touch land and run. She focused on the song of creaking of ropes and the calls of crew members securing the boat.

This short diversion had been intended as a reprieve, a quiet space between past fear and future uncertainty. Instead, it felt like a wrong move, a fatalistic misstep, the pivot that could send her careening away from her slim chance at a new life—at new lives.

She rose with practiced nonchalance as her nerves pulled taut enough to hum under her skin. She smoothed her shirt over the hidden papers cradled next to her heart, steadied herself against the rail, and prepared to step off into the sterile anonymity of the city. She scanned the park as they neared. The normal amount of guards, the normal amount of surveillance. Still, a warning pinged in her blood. The ferry bumped into the dock, signaling her arrival back to land.

The crew members quickly secured ropes and announced the arrival, guiding passengers to a single exit. A sturdy metal ramp was firmly anchored to bridge the gap between ferry and dock. The passengers were silent as they disembarked, the hollow echo of their footsteps the only evidence of their passing. As soon as she felt solid ground, she felt a shudder go through her. She was almost free, just a 10 minute walk away from the Fulton Street station. The blood thrummed in her ears.

Three steps forward, and then out of nowhere a park ranger was pulling her aside. There was no polite 'ma'am' this time. She was pulled to the side, and a phone was held up to her face. On a video call, the face of the museum guard was looking back at her, a deep sorrow shining from his eyes. He looked away.

"That her?" asked the ranger holding her elbow. Several more men in uniform had appeared out of nowhere to grab her, pull her purse away and pin her hands behind her. Their hands were on her, feeling through her clothes, feeling the secret curves under her clothes. A hand slipped into her shirt, bypassing the envelope to explore freely before pulling it free.

"Yea, that's her," said the museum guard. The screen went dark.

"Looks like we got one," crowed the ranger as he put the phone away. "Bring her down, boys!"

Glenda's feet were kicked out from under her and she fell like a stone. She barely noticed the sting of her flesh against pavement. Her jacket was ripped off, her shirt untucked and she could feel her skirt hiked up too high to be appropriate in the struggle.

"What are these? Planning to go somewhere?"

Her worn out envelope was waved in her face.

"I was approved... research trip. It is all legal." She was openly sobbing now, her breath coming in short, panicked gusts.

"I call bullshit," said a voice from above. "She was trying to run."

"America not good enough for you? Answer me!" Someone kicked her in the stomach. She lay gasping, unable to speak, a dying fish on dry land.

"Can't speak English."

"Roger, good enough. These papers were stolen. Take her."

Glenda didn't have enough breath to scream. Through her tears she saw the Statue she had risked everything to see, like her great-grandmother before her, shining brightly.

The final words of the false promise came back to her as they pulled Glenda to her feet, zip tied her hands behind her, tore her blouse, and heaved her into the back of a waiting van.

I lift my lamp beside the golden door…

The doors slammed closed, abandoning Glenda to darkness.

VELVET BAG

SHANE DAVID MORIN

There's a courthouse in town. Tucked away among domestic
violence and
Child abandonment files there's a folder filled with failures, to
thrive, to drive
Halfway between one residence and the next. In the folder are
papers (certified mind you)

True attesting that single dads aren't as villainous as mother's
"deadbeat" plea, that fabricated accusations are as tar and
feather. Motions state:
Parent A shall run, play, entertain and love child, on weekends
only, Fridays at 4PM through Sundays at 2PM, with school
vacations open to more time, as mother sees fits.
Not realizing that alienation isn't just an ET occurrence. See,
My Monday-Friday is just burning time until the 45-minute
drive arrives like a long-awaited
Christmas gift. Forgive me (or don't) for saying so, but I'd rather
ingest ether than behold mother's face, she who concocts
fictions, shatters time at a whim, seeks surrogate dads for child.

Every Friday is a slow deviation from humanity, Bell Standard

incapacitated, petrified at perversions of love, mother's form
sloughs as imperfect skin, each shedding
A new iteration of evil. Eyes once honeyed, meld to vermillion
slits. Black arachnid tail lashes out, a new addition to vitriolic
arsenal, tip curls lazily above head, drips clouded venom.
Bostonian voice subsists in hisses, kisses daughter goodbye, we
drive for miles and miles,
Daughter's smile a mask of serenity. This won't last. It never
does. Sundays arrive like an atomic flash, blindingly destructive,
the shockwaves pervading the rest of the week. Drop offs at
mom's are sacrificial, daughter lays prostrate at mother's altar, a
weekly feast of fear. I drive the miles home, all pursuits of
happiness left at the doorstep with Daughter for one more week.

I'd capture all the stars for Daughter, scoop them
In an infinite net, collect them in a velvet bag,
Gift them for a simple smile, witness her snuggle
Alpha Canis Majoris for warmth. But, I'll settle

For a simple text back, a requited hug, a "love you too,"
To shape this universe I call home.

FIRST PERSON, SHOOTER

ROCKY COLAVITO

The path to a happy life goes right through college; a four-year degree is your ticket to prosperity, status, and success. Don't wait; apply today. See your guidance counselor for help!

"Test, Test, Test. Okay, that works; I sure would hate for the play-by-play of this bit of uncivil disobedience to go unrecorded. Video streaming is old hat, and in this case may get mistaken for a game. I want everyone to understand what's in my head so you know exactly why I'm making this particular choice. It's a long story, but it's not uncomplicated. There will be other versions, I am sure, but this is straight from the mouth of the perpetrator.

"And I'm a very straight shooter. Heh! Heh!

"If you find my wrenching humor out of a decidedly unfunny situation, that's a you problem. The culmination of events that have driven me to this are so juicily ironic that they would make Kafka jealous. Indeed, many's the time I've wondered if Kafka had taken over the pen in writing the story of my life.

"This is me taking it back. I've got this voice recorder jury rigged to WIFI and that WIFI is sending the dulcet tones of my voice to several voice transcription programs on different computers.

Don't ask how I did that, you wouldn't understand, and, to be honest, I'm not sure I fully understand how I did it myself. I'd originally wanted to do it so I could record lectures—rumor has it that professors can go in and edit them before they are published on the Learning Management System—but given the circumstances that are about to unfold, I have found another use for it. I am decisively taking back the control of my personal narrative. I already know the ending, just as you will, but what you may not know is what brought me to this. You'll hear some strange noises while I recount the lies that comprised my life up to this point. That's just me getting ready.

"I guess the story begins when I slipped out of my mother's womb and into the hands of the doctor who hung me by my heels and slapped my greasy red ass. I guess I cried; I was able to watch the video at the wrong age. Not sure an eight-year-old should be allowed to see his mother's bloated, splayed, and unshaven pussy, but that was that. I know I cried, squalled, kicked, and batted at my mother's tear-stained face when they put me on her chest. My thumb went into my mouth and I calmed down.

"Such a beautiful baby, such a smart baby, you are ready to do great things." My mother cooed to me, caught by the sound of the video.

If you're wondering where my father was, he was holding the video camera. He liked holding the video camera.

You're gonna go to the best colleges and have the best experiences son. But be sure that you put as much of your effort into getting ready for that next step. Everything you do going forward has bearing on what you become in the future. We'll help guide you however we can, but the mechanisms for success lie within your ability to study hard and master the material.

Anyway, my supposedly typical childhood revolved around the usual milestones that are characteristic of developing babies. First wobbly stand up, first steps, first successful trip to the bathroom, I won't bore you with a recitation. But out of all those milestones, what I remember the most is being read to. Mom and dad were both complicit here. They would read me picture books, newspaper comics, the backs of cereal boxes, whatever was handy. And inevitably one of them would coo 'this is learning, baby boy, it's important for success in your later life.'

It's all a process, baby boy. The tentative steps you take reflect the same ones you'll master as you move through all the learning that is to come. Stay the course, focus on becoming smarter, working harder, and pushing further. It will all pay off in the end.

And there you have it, a concerted effort to guide me on the path to success through learning. What a load of shit.

It continued through school, teachers kept harping on strange concepts like aggregation of skills, cognitive acuity, cumulative learning, all of which were linked to better preparation for the next year. I learned quickly that I would be rewarded for every grade of A that I got, and, like a Pavlovian pooch, I answered that bell. I did the work and asked for extra credit; I went to school when I was sick because I didn't want to miss anything. I actually studied the way that the teachers recommended, reviewing the day's notes after finishing homework assignments. I even worked in time for pleasure reading and daily journaling to keep my memory sharp. Being a good student got in the way of having friendships, and I learned about how the intelligent were viewed when my schoolmates fussed at me for blowing the curve.

College material . . . academic awards . . . could try harder . . . much better . . .this is a clearer indicator of your potential . . . fucking bright boy, blow the curve . . . they're just jealous of your intelligence sweetheart . . . you should enter this contest, it will look good on your college applications . . . did you write your application essay yet?

Fussing at me is a gentle way of saying that I ran home from school most days, barely keeping ahead of the pursuing bullies. My parents were of the mindset that violence is unnecessary, that turning the other cheek is a virtue, and that handling bullies is best done intellectually.

They were wrong, dead wrong. I still hear the voices of those motherfuckers every so often, chanting about my glasses, my tendency to wear sweater vests (with an occasional bow tie), my chain store tennis shoes, and my supposed polishing of the teachers' apples (if I remember correctly they used the words 'knob' or 'starfish'—my parents were shocked and did not tell me what those words meant initially—but I found out).

Fucking four-eyes . . . Sheldon looking pussy . . . how does the teacher's shit taste, starfish scraper?

The only thing that I knew was what I'd been told by my extended family and the teachers: learning is lifelong and will ultimately set you free.

The dirty fuckers lied, every single one!

Well, you're about to find out how that turned out.

High school was slightly better because it was the first time I was able to find a community of people like myself—suckers who swallowed the litany of lies about preparing for the future and the number of doors that would magically open when you walked out of college—can't forget that—with high grades and a plethora of relevant experiences. I joined the Academic Decathlon team, robotics club, and various book clubs, was selected for the National Honor Society, and had perfect attendance at all events for college bound students. I asked the right questions at these events, had regular meetings with the guidance counselor, and sought mentoring from my favorite teachers. I did everything that I was supposed to do.

Maybe it's time to try what you're NOT supposed to do!

And look where it's gotten me, sitting cross legged on my dorm room floor, and getting ready for the next step.

Doesn't it feel much better though? Doesn't personal autonomy give you a chubby?

My first failure was not being valedictorian of my graduating class; it wasn't a letdown for my parents, who were happy with the fact that I was one of four salutatorians, but it nearly destroyed me. Everything that I'd worked for was that particular point, and even though I'd already accepted admission to my first choice of college I spent the whole summer before my first year worrying that they would rescind my acceptance because of that misstep. It didn't happen, but the wound festered. And the fact that she went to the same school, a smaller midwestern private institution with a glittering reputation for placing its graduates, didn't help matters.

You should have gone somewhere else; this shithole just perpetuated all that bullshit that you got filled with. They're as much to blame as everyone else, especially your parents.

I arrived on campus ready to take the fight to the curriculum, inquiring as to which teachers were the most rigorous, and determined to show them how brilliant I was by enrolling in their classes. I resolved to let my work speak for itself, and not partaking in what my tormentors had called 'knob polishing.' But all through my experience I fixated on the hidden curriculum of job placement as the prize to be won. At every turn I was bombarded with subliminal, and not so subliminal, messages about how to play the end game of getting the best job. If it wasn't coming from the faculty themselves or the other students, it came from the disembodied voices of successful alumni which adorned posters outside of every department. They'd speak through printed letters, but the noxious gushing about the institution was painfully clear through the tone of the word choice.

"I wouldn't be where I am today without the support I found at . . ." "My classes were more than just learning and making friends, they taught me how to be a success in my career" "I am a better person, and a better contributor, because of my time at . . ."

It got so loud that I needed to get away from it, and that is when I found my niche in video game theory.

It was a new program that had been granted placement in the undergraduate curriculum. It was a cross disciplinary major that was housed in the Department of Popular Culture, but required courses in computer design, esports, military history, narrative theory, and visual rhetoric, among others. It seemed a natural choice for someone like me who had always been good at seeing how the pieces fit together. And handling the disparate, yet converging, strands of study was a good challenge. I declared my major at the end of my first semester.

See how the zombies' heads explode? This might be fun to try to apply elsewhere.

One of the nice things about the major was that it was refreshingly free of the noise about obtaining gainful employment. There was a lot of theory in the classes; and the practical side of things, while covered, was not at the forefront. I learned more about how things worked and why certain choices were made. The voices in my head quieted, for a time.

See how the game unfolds? What can you take from deconstructing this way of world making?

It was at the beginning of my third year when the voices came back, so loud that they kept me awake at night. It started with a new program at the beginning of the year that was part of the first day of classes. To make it successful the departments said that we had to go to check a new box in our undergraduate curricula. I went with a fully charged phone intending to spend most of the time playing one of the video games I'd become enamored of. It meshed my favorite movie genre—zombie apocalypse—with first-person perspective of a forager trying to stay alive in the face of incalculable odds against. Part of the foraging was obtaining weapons, and ammunition.

I had settled into a seat way up on the balcony of the auditorium when the provost walked on to the stage and introduced the event.

"Welcome one and all to the debut of what we expect will be an informative and enlightening experience for all of you. Today we are blessed with visits from successful alumni, representing the classes of 1959, 1968, 1974, 1984, 1997, 2006, and 2021, who will be talking with you about how their experience has shaped their working lives. They will offer valuable insights about acing that job interview, navigating the challenging new markets, and succeeding at your jobs. We pride ourselves on our ninety nine percent placement rate and look forward to you all eventually becoming part of that ninety-nine percent."

She prattled on to introduce the panelists, some of whom took seats on the stage, others were projected on huge viewing screens as they appeared via videoconferencing. And then it started:

The biggest thing I learned that helped me in my job . . . the one piece of advice I'd give every undergraduate . . . it's a game, there are rules, and you need to know them . . . I never felt bad when

I could say I did my best at trying to learn more than was expected . . . your required reading doesn't end after your last classes . . .

I dropped my phone at my feet, clapped my hands over my ears, and uttered a series of sounds that I later was informed sounded like a pained kitten. Two ushers appeared and escorted me out, conveying me to the campus health center.

"What happened? Are you on any medication that you might have forgotten to take? Has this ever happened before? Is there someone you need us to call?" The rapid fire questioning almost drowned me. I suddenly felt like I couldn't breathe.

That shit is smothering you; get some fresh air!

That earned me a trip to the hospital and a forty-eight-hour observation since it was late in the week. My parents arrived from one state to the east and hovered in my room, trading off stroking my hand and comforting me as if I were an infant as I thrashed on the bed, begging for ear plugs to counteract something only I could hear.

Work harder . . . get your shit together . . . you can't afford to let a set back like this check your progress . . . get your shit together . . . get your shit together . . . GET YOUR SHIT TOGETHER!!!!!!

I finally regained a modicum of coherence; at least enough to concoct a cover story.

Here's what you need to tell them . . .

"I honestly don't know what came over me. It was as if my hearing suddenly became so acute that everything sounded like feedback. It was piercing, drilling through both of my eardrums and colliding in my brain."

I avowed that it wasn't an issue now, swore that I had not been playing things too loud when I was wearing ear buds, and agreed to see an audiologist and inform medical professionals if it ever happened again. I was released, and arrived on campus in the middle of the first week of classes with the requisite doctors' notes and letters that allowed me free rein to leave class if I needed to, access to course recordings, and permission to wear sunglasses since it was presumed that bright lights had exacerbated my problem.

I was surprised at how easily the duplicity came to me. But unfortunately, I still had the dissonance bearing drum thumping about post college success to deal with. And it was everywhere.

Get the inside skinny on how to ace that job interview . . . ten tips for presenting a killer resume . . . keywording is the new must have skill . . . how to plow through the virtual job search . . . job . . . success . . . money . . . status . . . kill Kill Kill KILL KILL!

The forums that set off my breakdown became monthly occurrences, accompanied by expectations of attending them and journaling about them. The institution mandated attending two of these events for every year of attendance, with half of these being forums with graduates who were in your chosen field of study. My queries about which graduates were a best fit for me since I was in one of the campuses newest majors were met with bored looks and impatience. "Look for people who are working in media" or "I'll have to get back to you on this," or even, "do you know of any graduates to suggest as someone to invite?" were their attempts at helping. I had an idea of who we should invite, but Marcus Mayfield, the infamous cult leader whose followers were wiped out in a showdown with government agents was long dead. The school never lists him among its graduates, but he's a great example of someone who used a rhetoric degree for its intended purpose.

My name is Marcus Mayfield, and I know just how you feel; you and I are a lot alike, outliers, shunned, bullied, harassed, wear the wrong clothes or follow the wrong interests. But I have found workarounds for all that dissonance, and I want to help you create those of your own. It's not as hard as you might think, and you are probably already doing some of the things that will help you build the workaround strategies. And the best thing is, you're not the only one out there, and there are many more folks like yourself than you might believe.

The first time I made that suggestion I intended it as a joke; the minion I suggested it to didn't find it funny. So, in acts of learning place anarchy, I used fake email accounts and burner phones to flood the Office of Alumni and University Relations with the same suggestion. It was fun for a time until the school newspaper got wind of my little joke and published a story on it. I cooled my jets and found workarounds for attending the alumni forums. I had better things to do with my time.

Who is this mysterious on-line presence that has caused the email and social media accounts of Alumni and University Relations to crash from the onslaught of requests to bring a dead man, whose connection to the school is tenuous at best. AUR is adamant in resisting these entreaties, indicating that the suggested speaker has little to contribute to campus conversations and nothing that would be of value to anyone attending the institution.

By the time senior year began I was looking forward to finishing and putting my skills to work. My senior project was coming together swimmingly. I'd envisioned a whole game universe where the first person was enmeshed in different types of social and conflict situations; it was inspired by a television show about this scientist who found himself "jumping" into different people at different points along the time continuum. I dumped the historical angle, saving that for new versions, and focused on situations in contemporary time. For example, at the click of a mouse the player could find him or herself in a professional wrestling match against a reigning world champion —I created different personae based on existing wrestlers. Or, someone could find themselves as a guest at the Academy Awards, or a high fashion show, or a senior prom—this last one would be popular for people like myself who didn't attend theirs. It allowed players to test their abilities to fit in to these situations and used an algorithm to assess how the choices would fare. I saw it as both a learning and entertainment tool. The base version that I used to "sell" the product in our competition was one that put the player in a job interview situation. I figured that focus would align with the corporate aims of the school.

I called it "Vicarious Reality"; I thought it would be a hit.

Since you haven't heard of it you must know that it wasn't. The panel of judges liked the idea and the execution but wondered how it would be marketed and if people would be willing to fork over the money to, as one person snarkily said, play dress up. I argued that I'd market it like a new illicit drug, the first taste— which would be the job interview—would be free, and the other experiences would be add-ons. My vision included different programs involving different historical periods, and movies and television shows, which would be developed as we ran the shakedown cruise of the first version.

They weren't buying what I was selling; my proposal didn't even place in the top three.

Sorry, but we just can't see how anyone would buy this when there are free resources for doing mock interviews through college campuses and local organizations. What you're suggesting is that situations like this are games; they aren't. The ability to effectively play a game is no help in trying to obtain a job.

It was enough to allow me to graduate, but it was not the ticket to industry success. And that is when the pressure got more intense.

"Do you have any interviews lined up?" my faculty advisor asked me when I went in to discuss my last semester of classes.

"No, I'm still looking. Why is this a problem?"

"Well, as a new program we do have institutional expectations. You are aware of the university's job placement record, right?"

"I've heard about it," I said, dreading what was to come.

"Well, it makes the program look bad if we can't get all of our new graduates employed."

I wanted to scream "How is this my problem?" or "Fuck the university's expectations sideways!" but the conversation proved what I had come to suspect. The students here are only statistics that the university can point to and chest thump.

Look, we have a really high placement rate. See, an education here is the ticket to gainful employment. Come here, and the American Dream's pursuit of happiness, via a great job, will be at your feet.

The voices in my head started again, a choir of dissonance. I held it together through the advising appointment, left with a handful of brochures about companies that would be looking to hire people, and returned to my room. I threw the literature in the wastebasket, flopped on my bed, and put the pillow over my face. I was not trying to smother myself; I was seeking to muffle the chants and rhymes about what becomes of those who don't buy into the company line.

Don't be a schmo, off to work you go! . . . A job in the hand and life will be grand. . . . A degree from us means you don't ride the bus.

This was the crossroads that I lingered at, and I was too depleted to decide on direction yet. I decided to use the Christmas break to try and concoct a plan. I knew my parents would be interested in my answers, even though we had decided to take a two-week cruise to some warm weather climate. It was designed to not only celebrate the holiday, but also my impending graduation.

I spent it in a fog, partially due to unforeseen seasickness on my part, but mostly due to the fact that I couldn't shut the voices off. In between bouts of nausea either in the stateroom toilet or over the side of the ship I was bombarded with the voices who had started to imitate my advisor, professors, and the people on those confounded alumni forums.

I'm here for whatever help you need . . . stop by during office hours, I have a lead for you . . . if you need a reference, please let me know . . . have you registered for the job fair in January? . . . here's a list of new resources the Career Center is offering for graduating seniors . . . graduating . . . job search . . . interviews . . . . proper dress . . . time is flying . . . the end of the semester . . . the end of the semester . . . the end . . .

It was all I could do to not throw myself over the railing, or jam chopsticks into my ears at the Asian buffet on the ship. My parents were quite worried, and didn't feel that the ship's doctors were equipped to handle my condition. It was decided that we would cut the cruise short and fly back home at one of the stops. I was cleared to fly before we disembarked and spent the flight in the bliss of some very potent sleeping pills. It was the first good night's sleep I'd had in weeks.

A nd I was gifted with a new vision for what I was going to do.

It's time for you to make some noise, drown out their advice, make them listen to yours if it's the last thing they do. Your game is the basis, but it needs some modification . . .

Upon our return home I immediately went to my room and drafted a plan for a newer version of Vicarious Reality. It would be a heretofore unexplored simulation, drawing from the most popular first-person games on the market, as well as popular entertainment and current events. When my folks asked about it, I told them about the older version. They were suitably impressed. And I congratulated myself on the snow job.

I spent the rest of Christmas break in isolation, designing, coding, building the new world. I had a working model by the time I was supposed to go back to school. I was pleased with myself, but that feeling would be short lived.

What I discovered upon my return was that someone had pirated my initial design and given it to the school. It was my own fault for making the draft version free; I had unknowingly provided the template for something that was now available for every student through the Office of Student Success. It was pre-installed on our landing pages and downloading the app was made mandatory. I was welcomed back to each of my four classes that I needed to graduate with assignments linked to doing a practice interview for each class and writing up the experience. So, not only did I have to play the institution's game in order to graduate, but I had to do it knowing that I was using something that was my design that had been rejected by the committee, only to see it in use every time I turned on my computer or my phone.

Those dirty motherfucking thieves; I thought this idea wasn't promising, you and your lies about hard work being for yourself. You meant for YOURselves, didn't you? This will not stand, nosirree bob, it must be answered.

Now you're talking; start planning your answer.

A lesser person would have collapsed; I found the resolve to muscle through, spending all my time on perfecting the new version. My grades suffered, but I didn't care. My advisor summoned me to talk about my falling grades, telling me that I was in danger of falling off the dean's list, which would inhibit my job possibilities. I told him that I was diligently working on a project that I could use as part of a job interview, since I had already been told that the job interview function was now the property of the school based on a rarely invoked clause saying that the university owned anything that was created via university support.

Instead of making me angrier, that clause made me smile. The irony was going to be delicious.

I managed to fake my way through the job interviews, treating them as if they were jobs that I really didn't want. My professors didn't find my humor appropriate but passed me since failing a graduating senior would affect the school negatively. By the end of finals, I had perfected the new version. It just needed one more component.

Today I'll supply that component. It's graduation day and I'm decked out in my vestments, no fancy stoles indicating Dean's List or academic honors. Nothing on my mortar board showing where I would be working after graduation. Just a generic graduate in a sea of honorees. My only accoutrements are the handicam attached to my shoulder, and something under the folds of my graduation gown.

The ceremony was held in the huge auditorium that had hosted everything from touring Broadway shows to the tapings of college bowl quiz shows. I was giddy with anticipation, mentally hurrying up the endless parade of speakers who, surprise, all exhorted us to become gainfully employed, which would be the key to lifelong happiness. I picked up little asides to the few of us who weren't "gainfully employed"; the insinuations being that we were besmirching the reputation of the fine institution that was about to confer degrees on us. It set my guts roiling and my ire rising. I reached through a slit I had cut in my robe and touched my pacifier.

He's talking about you; shut that fucker up!

My row finally stood to walk to the stage to receive our degrees. It was hard to contain my enthusiasm as the line seemed to take forever. I reached the bottom step and once again stroked my pacifier. I released it from its confines when my feet hit the stage.

The provost stood in front of me, all smiles with an extended hand. I walked toward her hiding my pacifier. When I clasped her hand, I shoved the pacifier into her belly and fired two silenced shots.

Fuck, you nearly blew her in two. Nice shootin', Tex!

The camera caught the pained look on her face and the gout of blood that shot out of her mouth. The screams heightened as her body fell, but nobody moved. I used the pause to sight the gun on the president's face. His head evaporated as the high-powered slug hit his mouth and exploded. I didn't wait to see him fall. I had an escape route plotted and ran for it, shooting people who got in my way. The valedictorian cowered before me; hands clenched pleadingly. I shot her in the crotch and gave the man who came to her aid the same treatment.

Whoa, right in the babymaker! Just as well.

I heard the sirens going off as I exited the auditorium through one of the side doors. A campus security vehicle skidded to a stop in front of the auditorium, loudspeaker blaring "Active Shooter, Shelter in Place!" The audience for graduation must have missed the memo; the security officer was trampled to death in the stampede from the building. I, on the other hand, made tracks to the first place that I had stashed more weapons. I ditched my cap and gown, pulled on a balaclava with a red skeleton's face, and dropped the pistol I'd used in favor of an uzi with four extra clips. I circled back to the milling crowd in front of the auditorium and opened fire.

Just like in the game, remember actually shooting the ducks in the barrel?

The bullets were of the variety known as cop-killers, designed to shoot through bullet stopping clothing. Since no one was wearing Kevlar, the effects upon human flesh were exhilarating. Faces disintegrating, guts distending from huge holes to be pulled out when they were stepped upon, limbs blown off, through and through shots hitting people in the second and third columns. By the time I'd emptied two clips people had started retreating, running pell-mell toward anywhere that might provide shelter.

I turned my attention to one of the police cars that had arrived. I fired at the gas tank; the cop killers did their nasty business and blew up the vehicle, splashing the officers who'd exited and several people who ran towards it with flaming gasoline. I turned away and laughed loudly as the figures forgot about stopping, dropping, and rolling, blundering into others and setting them aflame. Who knew that graduation gowns went up in flames so easily?

And there's your fireworks display! They're funny when they run!

I drew a bead on a group of people that I recognized. It was the committee who'd in all likelihood pirated my design and the credit for designing it. I shot all four of them in the legs, the bullets completely severed each of the legs at the knee or mid shin.

I speed walked to hover over the four people who were squirming in pain on the ground. I shoved the Uzi into the first one's mouth and shot a burst. The head exploded on three sides, coating the others with brains, blood, and bone. The chair of the committee was next; I shot him in the stomach and left him there looking dumbly at his splayed open abdomen and trying vainly to push his guts back into place.

A third tried to crawl away; it was too tempting to shoot him in the ass, and I succumbed. Of course, I just had to shove the barrel of the Uzi into the seat of his brown stained pants and fire off another burst. The victim's back blew up and split.

The last person was also the youngest, a newly hired professor who was just completing his first year. He quit trying to flee and worked himself to a seated position against the side of the building. He recognized me.

"Let me guess," he said, "you saw what we did with your original design."

"Yeah, but I've improved on it." I brandished the weapon and kept the camera glued to his face.

"Do tell, consider it a dying man's last request."

"Are you ready for your close up?" I asked.

He gasped, realizing exactly what I was doing.

"Adios, motherfucker." I snarled as I put one bullet through his throat. It nearly severed his head, which bent forward and hung tenuously by his shredded trachea.

I scanned the crowd looking for more potential victims, picking off random souls as they tried to sneak out of the venue thinking that the coast was clear. I kept moving, purposefully seeking some of the places where I had stashed other loaded weapons and ammunition, filming all the while. I don't know how I avoided encounters with the police, but I suspect that there were others in the crowds who somehow had acquired weapons that allowed me to hide in plain sight. I ditched the Uzi by the parking garage, grabbing a sniper's rifle and a backpack full of Teflon coated ammunition. I loaded the rifle, checked the load in my Colt .45, and took the elevator to the fifth floor of the parking garage.

I disabled the elevator and moved to a row of cars that I accessed by breaking the windows. I slipped several into neutral and pushed them toward the only ramp giving access. One by one I sent them down the ramp, letting them smash into the wall at the bottom and pile up. When I heard an engine ascending the ramp, I aimed the rifle at an exposed gas tank and fired.

The explosion took out the approaching car and gave me the opportunity to run to the second elevator and disable it. The third was all the way across the garage and by the time I reached it the doors were opening. I opened fire with the forty-five; cutting down three more campus police officers. I grabbed their weapons, disabled the elevator, and grabbed the one cop who was still breathing. I dragged him to the side, saw the massing group on the street below, and dumped him over the wall. He fell on three people, the bodies splattered like ripe fruit.

My son, my misbegotten son, thank you for listening to my voice, and thank you for giving it a forum. You have made me proud.

Thank you, Mr. Mayfield.

I went to work shoving more cars in front of the stair wells, then shot them as well. The fires would delay access, and I hoped that this would buy me enough time to finish this mission.

I verified that all the footage had been uploaded to my server, and I quickly crafted a cover letter that I would attach to the footage, the coding, and the instructions. I send everything to a mailing list of video game companies large and small, corporate and independent. Given the audience for first-person shooters, I hoped that at least one company would decide to put this game out.

I hunkered down as low as I could in the middle of the parking garage. I unclipped the handicam and pointed it at myself. I checked the remaining memory and found I had perhaps seven minutes of filming left. I took a breath and began.

"My name is ******, and until recently, I was a student here at ***** University. Coming here was supposed to be the next step in a life directed toward getting a good education because it was the key to lifelong happiness. It was a pile of lies designed to fill the hungry stomach of the beast with easy pickings to chew up and shit out. The happiness that comes from working hard and excelling is a pipe dream that blew up in the faces of many. The surviving graduates will be exploited just as they were when they attended, called upon to show out for good old U and speak of the contributions the institution has made to their lives and careers.

"My actions have colored that experience and have given me the basis for my capstone project. The original idea was stolen by the university and lives on its servers, allowing new generations of students to experience various aspects of the employment search and time on the job. You won't find my name attached to it, but I have sent the original designs and my development notes to several news publications, and the Board of Trustees and to the alumni database, along with a clear articulation of how this project was stolen by the institution.

"But that's water under the bridge; I've refined the original design to accommodate the vicarious interests of survivalists, the military, hunters, and even people who love Richard Connal's 'The Most Dangerous Game.' Campus Carnage, as I've chosen to call it, is in the hands of multiple video game companies; with actual footage shot by me during what will no doubt be called a 'mindless rampage.' Let me assure you it was far from mindless; I planned everything down to seconds, I walked the area depicted in the game, and I acted alone in committing the atrocities that fill the footage. I let this be my legacy to this representative of an educational system that has failed me and countless others.

"When a skyscraper is built upon a poor foundation, cracks will appear in the masonry, things may start sagging, and ultimately the structure will collapse in a heap, possibly killing hundreds. Collateral damage for the bill of goods sold by the colleges, their doting alums, and the social systems that lead us to believe that hard work and a good education is the key to lasting happiness.

"It's wrong on so many levels, and my time is short. Marcus Mayfield is one of the most famous graduates of this institution and yet you never hear about him because it's been determined that he is a poor representative of what a ***** education can produce. He is my inspiration, and it is my hope that I will rival his legacy with mine."

I turn the sniper's rifle toward myself and draw it slowly towards my mouth. I take a moment to utter one last set of words.

"The institution is just as much a cult as the one Mayfield formed, people attracted by charisma and empty promises. Ask them to admit that in my absence."

I push the barrel into my mouth, smile as best I can, and pull the trigger. My second to last vision is my blood and brains hitting the handicam.

My last vision is the figure of Marcus Mayfield, in his signature flowing crimson robe, arms outstretched, a smile on his face, waiting to receive me.

THE SOCIAL LOTTERY

XAVIER POE KANE

"I don't know what it was, but last year's winner had this face you just wanted to punch!" Peg Inman said as she sipped her mimosa over brunch with her sister-in-law.

"Absolutely!" Sandy agreed, sipping on a bloody mary. "I wonder why it's always some troll with their smug selfies. The secrets they keep from their friends and family—"

"And don't forget their kooky political opinions!" Peg chortled. "Remember last year's winner? Her college paper on the far-right radicals in the 1990s? The way she echoed their absolute fascism was cringeworthy!"

"Absolute cringe!" Sandy shuddered. "Don't forget the guy who won the year before her. What was his name?"

"Jerry Ellis!"

Sandy toasted Peg. "You're a trove of Lottery trivia! Jason and I really need to take you to trivia night with us next week! It's always a category the week after the drawing."

"Count me in!" Peg finished her drink and snapped her fingers until a waiter removed the empty glass and brought her another.

XAVIER POE KANE

"That Ellis guy, what a creep! And a moderate! One of those dead-center jerks who's too timid to actually pick a side. And another punchable face! Ever wonder why they always pick losers and jerks?" she asked, already tipsy enough to forget Sandy had asked the same question.

"Jason and I were talking about that last night." Sandy leaned back, looking ready to impart some wisdom. "You know how your brother loves his conspiracy podcasts?"

Peg nodded as she took another sip of her mimosa. "He's still listening to Joe Franklyn?"

Sandy nodded but not as dismissively as Peg would've liked. "We don't think it's as random as they say. Not every one of us is placed in the Lottery. It's only a select few—those who deserve to win. The rest of us good, decent folk are left out of it. Jason called it something … oh, what did he say?" Sandy furrowed her brow. "Oh, yeah! 'Culling the herd.' That's where you remove the undesirables, so the herd doesn't get contaminated by poor breeding."

Peg raised her glass. "Well, then I guess neither of us is ever going to win it!"

"Hear! Hear!" Sandy's lips twisted into a haughty grin as they clinked glasses. "Have you ever seen a winner in person?"

Peg shook her head. "No. But it's on my bucket list! I'd love to see one up close before I die."

Sandy glanced toward the vegan leather satchel lying on the table next to Peg's plate. "Is that your new tablet?"

The black tablet had become ubiquitous after the tumult of the late 2020s and into the even worse 2030s that almost destroyed the United States from the inside. It provided free internet and access to all the infotainment the masses could consume or desire.

Peg nodded proudly. "It's the latest tech from Beijing. 12K screen, C2VP Crystalline Reverb audio driver—my implants have never sounded better!"

"Well, can't have the next partner at your firm sporting old tech! What did you do with your old one? Recycled, I assume? Reselling is so gauche."

Peg's back stiffened with pride. "I donated it to the unhoused. Why not let those who have so little have *something*?"

"So true and so selfless!" Sandy's eyes narrowed as she looked at the new tablet once more. "That's a nice new charm." She indicated the large sapphire that dangled off a ribbon secured to the tablet, the light sparkling off its facets. "What happened to the one David got you when you got married?"

Peg blushed. "I forgot to take it off before donating it. I was heartbroken, and David was a little upset. He'd saved three months of his intern salary to pay for it! It was a lab-created gem, of course, since that was all he could afford at the time. But, when you're in love …" Her voice trailed as she thought of her fleeting youth.

P eg sat at her vanity, removing her makeup. Her husband David was already fast asleep. Like everyone else, he paid attention to the Lottery once a name was drawn every third of July, but he didn't follow it as closely as she did. Few people had the social consciousness to obsess over the tradition. She looked in the mirror, thinking just how *un*punchable her face was, and considered Sandy's theory about culling the herd. It made sense to her. After all, society would never allow someone of her caliber to be chosen! It was the scammers, spammers, and trolls who were a burden on its resources who always won. Wasn't that the point? To remove the undesirables?

"Good evening, America!" Summer Warner's sing-song voice cooed in Peg's ear.

The time had arrived for the Lottery Commission to announce this year's winner.

"Normally, this is the time we come online and tell you who this year's Social Lottery winner is. However, tonight the Commission has announced that the Lottery is being discontinued due to political pressure from far-center extremists. As everyone knows, the Social Lottery has been the glue that holds our society together. By uniting as a country for one day a year to cast blame on one person, all of our animosity for those who disagree with us could be forgotten, and we could spend this day directing all of it at one person—*one person who deserves it.*"

"Damn moderates!" Peg spat, her voice loud enough to make David stir in his sleep.

Warner continued: "As a reward for catching all the stones society could throw at them, exactly 24 hours after the announcement, they would be rewarded with their dream home, exempted from paying taxes, and given a monthly stipend that would keep them in the top 0.05% for the rest of their lives. However, radical moderates see the Lottery as cruel, and the Supreme Court has just ruled in their favor and discontinued this yearslong tradition."

Peg's shoulders slumped in disappointment. Each year, for at least a month beforehand, the internet would be focused on the drawing. Rumors would abound. And while the Lottery had been certified as random and every citizen over the age of 15 was automatically registered, the government had acknowledged that an AI program used an algorithm to skew the probability based on demographics to ensure that no single group or region would be overly represented year after year.

This year, rumor had it that Peg's state had been heavily favored to produce a winner, which had meant the chance to cross one more thing off her bucket list. Feeling defeated, she took a sleeping pill and crawled into bed next to her husband, who was once again snoring softly.

The braying of Peg's alarm woke her at 6:30 a.m. She reached for her phone and scrolled through social media. Her eyes went wide, and she was suddenly awake with the realization that her number of friends had jumped to 314,159,265.

"What the hell?" she asked her empty bedroom, her still sleep-addled mind wondering when she had had the time to accept so many requests.

Peg checked her privacy settings only to find they were locked, and a new feature called "auto-accept" had been added. She tried to disable it but could not, and she was instantly irritated at the possibility of a glitchy update being pushed while she slept. Her phone was exploding with unread messages, and she opened the first one.

"FUCK YOU!" it screamed at her.

She blocked the sender and opened another.

"GOOD RIDDANCE!"

Block.

"LOSER!"

She felt a tear run down her cheek at the vitriol. She pushed it out of her mind and slipped out of bed; a warm shower would wash away her disappointment at the cancellation and help her forget about the social media glitch. The water felt good, and the scent of her myrtle wood body wash put her in a trance. When she got out of the shower, still feeling a little peeved at the undeserved angry comments, she lit a stick of incense. Smelling the frankincense, she took a moment to meditate and center herself.

An hour later—and 15 minutes behind her regular routine—Peg was out the door and on her way to work.

"Hey!" called the piercing voice of the 8-year-old who lived next door. "It's Mrs. Inman! The cunt!"

Peg froze. She was shocked that such language had come from little Nancy. "Excuse me! Nancy, young ladies don't use that word! What would your mother–"

"Slut!" Nancy's older brother, Bill Jr., joined his sister on the sidewalk.

"Fuck off!" yelled David, the youngest.

Peg was stunned. "I'm going to tell your parents!" she shouted as she stepped toward the trio.

Nancy picked up a small rock and threw it at Peg.

"Ow!" Peg screeched.

Soon, Bill Jr. and David had followed Nancy's lead and began pelting her with whatever small stones they could find.

"Stop it!" Peg screamed as she began running down the sidewalk, the soles of her sneakers rapidly pounding the pavement.

The children began chasing her, shouting horrible curses and names at her. At some point, her bag slipped off her shoulder, and one of her heels tumbled out onto the pavement. Bill Jr. got to it first and lofted it high, his siblings jumping up and down in celebration at the trophy.

"Hey, Andre," Peg said cheerfully, trying to put the horrifying experience with the Bowers children behind her. "The usual, please!"

This had been her morning ritual almost every day since Andre began working here as a high school student. Now, her generous tips were helping him through college, and he was repaying her with extra shots of espresso.

But this morning he refused to look at her, just nodding as he made her regular. Only this time, instead of an extra shot of espresso, he spat in it. When he slid the cup toward her, she noticed it said "Karen" instead of "Peg."

She turned to ask the other customers if they'd seen it, but despite the normal morning rush, people weren't crowding her. Instead, it was as if she had developed a sudden onset of leprosy.

"Bitch," someone muttered.

Peg began to cry as she backed toward the door.

"You forgot your coffee, moron!" a woman said before grabbing the cup, flipping off the lid, and throwing the contents at Peg.

The shop broke into roaring laughter.

She closed her eyes, not wanting to know if Andre was part of the cackling horde cruelly tormenting her. She turned and broke into a run, choosing to head to the safety of her office rather than home.

A post-it note had been placed on her screen: "SEE ME NOW – BRIAN."

This brought a smile to her face, and she almost skipped to his office despite how difficult it was in only one heel. They had avoided hanky-panky at work, but once he heard about her bonkers of a morning? He would go ahead and take her on his desk just like they had joked about.

"You would not believe the morning–" Peg started as she stepped inside his office.

"Close the door," he growled.

It set her on edge. "Someone's in a rough mood today." She crossed the room and bent over his desk, giving him a view down her blouse.

"Sit down, slut," Brian replied, his gaze never leaving her eyes.

"Roleplaying? What am I? Your whore? A secretary with too many typos? A–"

"Will you shut the fuck up?" He slammed a fist on the desk. "I thought I knew you. I thought we were on the same team. Yeah, we've had our differences, but I never thought you were one of *those* people." He turned the monitor on his desk around so she could see.

Her name leaped out at her from the headline: "Peggy Inman, Far-Left Terrorist?" Her lips quivered as she read excerpts from a paper she had written in college about how both the leftist extremists in the 2020s and their far-right equivalents had brought the country to the brink of civil war and oblivion. The lines were cherry-picked and strewn together to paint her as radical.

"Brian, I never said that!"

"They posted the original paper with these passages highlighted, Peg." He turned and looked out the window, his back to her. "We're a well-regarded law firm. We represent many clients affiliated with the Democratic-Federalist Party. We represent many firms engaged in the work of protecting the environment and workers' rights. Everyone is nervous in this political environment about being seen as too far left. We can't have a radical as a junior partner."

A tear slid down her cheek. She had 18 years with the firm, and her goal of partnership had been just within her grasp. "But it's been announced."

"And the offer has been rescinded," he said cruelly, spinning around to face her.

"I'll work doubly hard! I'll show–"

"You're also fired, you ugly cow. Now get the fuck out of my office. Clean out your desk and get your ass out of the building." He turned his back on her once again.

Peg just sat there and started to sob.

Brian stepped toward her.

For a moment, she thought that he was coming to his senses, that the insanity that was gripping those around her—even strangers—had loosened its grip on her lover. When he cuffed her across the face, that momentary hope was shattered.

"Brian!" she shouted, rubbing her hot, angry cheek.

"I said get the fuck out of my office!" he repeated, seemingly oblivious to the fact that he had just assaulted her. He grabbed her by the arm and pulled her to her feet. "Clean out your desk," he yelled as he dragged her to the door and opened it, "and get your ass out of the building!"

The door slammed behind her, causing her to jump. She looked around at the paralegals, secretaries, and junior attorneys. They stared at her, frozen in shock.

"Did you see that?!" Peg shouted. "Brian assaulted me! Someone call security!"

"Sure thing, bitch," said one of the paralegals before picking up the phone.

Moments later, two security guards and a police officer were on their floor. "Mrs. Inman?" the cop asked.

"Yes. I want to file a complaint against my boss, Brian–"

"I'm Officer Shirley. I'm here to escort you out of the building."

"But Brian assaulted me!"

Officer Shirley shook his head. "Listen, we can do this the easy way or the hard way. My wife left me and took my dog and truck. So, I'm living a country song right now and wouldn't mind doing something the hard way—especially since no one is gonna care."

Peg looked around. No one was going to help her. Some of her co-workers were taking videos, but they were jovial, lacking the normal sense of outrage at such an obvious injustice. She quietly went to her desk, gathered her things, and followed the security guards and Officer Shirley out of the building.

Standing on the sidewalk, she felt cold despite the July heat. Her mascara now smudged and melting, she called for an Uber. The closest one pulled up to the curb but sped off just as she put her hand on the door. She hung her head and slowly started walking home, awkwardly limping in one shoe. The physical discomfort harmonized with the anguish of the morning's rejections.

———

A fter a long, degrading walk home, Peg stood before her front door. Safe if not entirely sound, she was ready to slip into a warm bath and even found herself hoping David might hold her. He would be home soon, and she had done some serious self-reflection on her forced walk home. She'd decided to admit her indiscretion against him and their marriage and then beg him to forgive her.

She opened the door and was greeted by piles of boxes that had not been there when she left for work. She heard rustling coming from the bedroom. "Honey? You're home early. You won't believe the day I've had." Peg paused to listen but heard no response. "David? Honey? That is you, right?"

She got to the open bedroom door and saw her husband ripping her clothes out of their closet and haphazardly tossing them into boxes.

"Fuck off, Peg."

"David," she felt tears starting to well, "what's going on?"

"I'm kicking you out."

"Wait? You're doing what?" She steadied herself on the door jamb. "Why?"

"First, you fucked Brian. He texted me, even had pictures." David tossed an expensive pair of heels into a box. "Then I saw what you've been saying about me and my mother on Messenger. Not to mention the insane political shit that's smeared across the news."

"You-you can't kick me out! I'm on the deed!"

"Guess what, Peg? No one cares. Want me to call the cops?"

The memory of her firing made her shudder, and she knew that the cops would not be on her side. Head hung in dejected shame, she turned and slowly made her way to the front door, stopping by the kitchen to grab a bottle of wine on her way out.

The afternoon passed in a blur. No matter where she went, she was a pariah. She forgot to grab a wine opener, so she stopped by a corner market to buy one. The store owner had pulled out his phone and showed her the pictures Brian had taken of her. They'd been uploaded to several porn sites.

"I don't want your money, but you can suck my cock for the cork*screw*." He ogled her and obscenely rubbed himself.

She turned and slunk out of the store.

"Uppity whore!" he yelled at her back.

Nowhere would serve her, so she began looking for an alley in which to drink her wine.

An unhoused man who stunk of cheap liquor and for whom it had been God knows how long since his last shower said, "Trade ya." He eyed her wine as he jiggled a bottle of the cheap red that the degenerates in fraternities and sororities drank more for its high alcohol percentage than its flavor.

She shrugged. "Why the fuck not?" She handed him the expensive bottle, took the cheap stuff, and curled up across from him. With a sigh, Peg tried not to think about the man's backwash as she took a swig. Then she surveyed her surroundings.

There were others here, and they all had their heads buried in what she assumed were donated tablets. Her assumption was confirmed when she spied a small familiar gem dangling from one's corner. The memory of happier times rushed back to her, causing her lips to start to turn up into a smile.

But better than nostalgia was the look on the woman's dirty, careworn face. Life and the elements had not been kind to her, and Peg could see the echoes of tragedy traced in the lines of her face. However, whatever the woman was looking at was bringing her joy. She was laughing and showing a friend some video, and Peg overheard bits and pieces about a happy childhood.

For the first time since waking up to all the social media hate and the events of the day, Peg smiled. She had done something good in this world after all.

A vile voice shattered the fleeting moment of solace. The woman using the tablet looked her up and down a few times before shouting: "It's her!"

Every head in the alley turned toward the woman who pointed at Peg, and then every head turned in unison toward her.

"I knew the skank smelled!" said the man she'd traded her wine with as he used a rusty multi-tool to open her bottle.

"Get the fuck outta here, bitch!" someone yelled from the back of the alley.

"Yeah!" the woman who'd recognized her echoed. "Leave us good folks alone! Go be with your own kind!"

An old tin can of baked beans suddenly bounced off her forehead, bean juice splattering across her face and hair.

Numb, she stood and left the alley as its inhabitants jeered at her.

After walking aimlessly for a good while, the sky opened up and the rain poured down upon her slumped and defeated form. Night fell, and eventually the harassment started to slack off, leaving her alone to process the new lens through which the world viewed her. She found herself missing the abuse. At least it was some degree of human interaction.

She had messaged her sister-in-law asking about the update to her social media and telling her about all the insanity.

Sandy responded. "You are a dumb broad. For someone who knows so much about the Lottery, it's taking a God-awful long time for you to figure this out."

She, Peg Inman, had been selected as this year's sacrifice. Her destruction would be the glue that kept society together. For months after, the tribes would put their differences aside. Because of her carefully cherry-picked writings from college, her tribe would be reminded that it, too, could harbor radicals. The other tribe would have their blood lust sated, just like she had last year when another woman had been sacrificed. Peg had cheered when that woman, whose name now escaped her memory, splattered her brains on national TV.

She suddenly heard the sound of helicopter blades followed by the sight of a blinding spotlight. At first, she thought it might be the police, that someone in her life might have decided to force the authorities to save her from herself. She held up her hand to shield her eyes and noticed the helicopter was from the ANWR Network, the streaming channel Summer Warner worked for.

At this point, Peg looked around her. Her drunken feet had brought her to a bridge over the Mississippi River. She stood at the midpoint and looked down at the dark water churning beneath her. She put one leg over the side and then swung over the other. Her pain would be over soon. A line from a story she had read in a 20th Century American Literature course popped into mind. "Corn be heavy soon," she whispered. "I hope it's worth it."

As she pushed off the bridge, her watch beeped midnight, and Peg Inman laughed. The last thing she saw was a fleeting glimpse of a maniacally giggling face reflected in the dark mirror of the water.

She'd finally seen a Lottery winner in person.

S ummer Warner stared at the camera in a little bit of shock. "Well, folks," she collected herself, "she made it until midnight—the first Lottery winner to actually still be alive at the start of a new day. The closest was John Trotter six years ago, who lasted until 11:47 p.m. A testament to Mrs. Inman's inner strength—even if she did have a really punchable face. Another Lottery is over, and another reminder that extremism in pursuit of virtue is a vice."

364 Days Later …

The small black tablet connected to the implant in your ear canal momentarily draws your attention away from your evening routine. The time has arrived for the Social Lottery Commission to announce this year's winner.

"Good evening, America!" Summer Warner's sing-song voice coos in your ear. "Normally, this is the time we come online and tell you who this year's Social Lottery winner is. However, tonight the Commission has announced that the Lottery is being discontinued due to political pressure from far-center extremists. As everyone knows, the Social Lottery has been the glue that holds our society together. By uniting as a country for one day a year to cast blame on one person, all of our animosity for those who disagree with us could be forgotten, and we could spend this day directing all of it at one person—*one person who deserves it.*"

Warner continues: "As a reward for catching all the stones society could throw at them, exactly 24 hours after the announcement, they would be rewarded with their dream home, exempted from paying taxes, and given a monthly stipend that would keep them in the top 0.05% for the rest of their lives. However, radical moderates see the Lottery as cruel, and the

Supreme Court has just ruled in their favor and discontinued this yearslong tradition."

ABOUT THE EDITOR

Amanda Worthington is a writer of all things dark and perverse. She is particularly fond of psychological and cosmic horror and the ways ordinary humans behave in the face of adversity. Admittedly, much of her own work is semi-autobiographical. With a style that has been described as lyrical and immersive, she has been published in *Space & Time*, *Siren's Call*, and *Carnage House*. Amanda also founded Horror in the Heartland, the Heartland chapter of the HWA. When she's not writing or chaptering, she's probably hiking or cooking or playing Zelda. She lives in Kansas City with her two furry overlords Apollo and Artemis.

 facebook.com/HeldTogetherByCosmicGlue84

ABOUT THE ARTIST

Lynne Hansen is a horror artist who specializes in book covers. Her art has appeared on the cover of the legendary Weird Tales Magazine, and she was selected by Bram Stoker's great-grandnephew to create the cover for the 125th Anniversary Edition of Dracula. Her clients include Valancourt Books, Cemetery Dance Publications, Thunderstorm Books and Raw Dog Screaming Press. She has illustrated works by New York Times bestselling authors including Stephen King, Jonathan Maberry, Brian Keene, and Christopher Golden. Her art has been commissioned and collected throughout the United States and overseas. For more information, visit LynneHansenArt.com.

ABOUT THE AUTHORS

K.M. Bennett ("Mrs. Merriweather's Lactation Services") crafts stories with sparkle, splatter, and female rage. Her horror has been featured in several podcasts, including the *NoSleep Podcast*, *Thirteen* podcast, and more. She recently released her first solo short story collection, *Dreadful Dozen: Twelve Tales of Horror*. During the day, she works as a technical editor. She lives with her husband, two kids, and two rescue dogs. You can learn more at ThatKatieLady.com or stay in touch with her newsletter at substack.com/@kmbennett.

TK Brave ("Capitalism Kisses Your Self-Care Commodified Smile into Cash") writes poetry about the pursuit of survival while slinging shade at the emotional manipulation machinations of modern marketing.

Anton Cancre ("The First Law - Unbendable until Snapped") has hyperfocus obsession issues and is far too angry for such a cutie patootie. They're also a luddite who still has a blogspot website (antoncancre.blogspot.com). Pronouns: Any/All/Just Not Late For Dinner

J. Rocky Colavito ("First Person Shooter") calls himself "One of the last of the Generalists" because his career has offered him the opportunity to teach everything from first-year writing to graduate seminars on rhetorical theory. He's reinvented himself as an academic three times, moving from film studies, to cultural studies, to his last reinvention, horror writing. His horror inspirations run the gamut from Kaiju films to the newly resurrected splatterpunk movement.

His writing meshes his academic interests with horror tropes and settings, drawing upon professional wrestling, the giallo, tattoo artistry, food, creature features, the pornographic film industry, and cryptozoology as inspirations for horror pieces in all lengths and shapes.

And yes, he's the one they warned you about!

Dan B. Fierce ("Natural Selection") loves humor and horror alike, and many things in between. He has over twenty years of experience writing stand-up and sketch comedy and over 10 years of competitive creative writing in online forums. He has also had some opinion pieces published in *KC Lifestyles Magazine*, and several short stories published in various anthologies, as well as two solo releases.

He resides in the Kansas City, Missouri area with his long-time partner and husband.

Lindsey Beth Goddard ("The Traveling Freak Show") is an author of dark fiction, poetry, and true crime, living in Missouri, whose short stories have been published in e-zines such as *Gamut Magazine*, as well as in anthologies such as *Error Code* (Rabid Otter Horror). Her work has been performed on popular podcasts like *Creepy Podcast* and *Chilling Tales for Dark Nights*. She is the author of four short story collections, two poetry books, and a novel, *Ashes of Another Life*. For more information on her writing, visit: LindseyBethGoddard.com

Austin Gragg ("Feeding America") (they/he) is a queer writer, poet, and stay-at-home dad. They've been a finalist and multi-silver honorable mention in the Writers of the Future Contest and *Publishers Weekly* has praised Austin's dark fantasy as "decadent". Austin spent four years at the venerable *Space & Time Magazine* (Est. 1966) and closed their time there as editor-in-chief.

Formerly, Austin was a public librarian, digital literacy instructor, and technologist in public education. They live in their hometown of Independence, MO with their partner of fourteen years, two daughters, four cats, and three ferocious New Caledonian geckos.

When they aren't writing or reading, Austin studies the sword (Historical European Martial Arts) and plays tabletop games.

Larry Hinkle ("Company Policy") is the least famous author you've never heard of. A copywriter living with his wife and two doggos in Rockville, Maryland, when he's not writing stories that scare people into peeing their pants, he writes ads that scare people into buying adult diapers, so they're not caught peeing their pants.

His cosmic horror novella, *The Eris Ridge Trail*, was released to great reviews in March 2025, while his debut collection, *The Space Between*, was published in February 2024. His work has also appeared in *The Rack: Stories Inspired by Vintage Horror Paperbacks*; *October Screams: A Halloween Anthology*; and multiple times on *The NoSleep Podcast*, among others.

He's an active member of the HWA (his short stories made the preliminary Stoker ballot in 2020 and 2022); a graduate of Fright Club and Crystal Lake's Author's Journey short story and novella programs; an HWA mentee; and a survivor of the Borderlands Writers Bootcamp.

Stop by and visit him at thatscarylarry.com or stalk him on the socials at @thatscarylarry.

Ken Hueler ("Counting Sheep") teaches kung fu in the San Francisco Bay Area. His work has appeared in *Weirdbook*, *The Sirens Call*, *Weekly Mystery Magazine*, *Andromeda Spaceways*, and anthologies such as *The Cozy Cosmic* and *The Best of Carnage House Year One*. He is an assistant editor at *Space & Time* magazine and, with Frances Lu Pai Ippolito, co-edited the game fiction anthology *Winding Paths: A Playable Reading Experience.* You can learn more at: kenhueler.wordpress.com

Still not a best-selling author, **Xavier Poe Kane** ("The Social Lottery") is a former door gunner on the International Space Station. When not making the galaxy safe for democracy, he writes whatever weirdness comes to mind. He currently lives in the woods with his wife, Morticia, in a state of mutual weirdness with their dogs Chuck Norris and the three-legged Jabba the Hutt. Thanks to the GI Bill, he has a MFA in Popular Fiction Writing & Publishing from Emerson College.

Joe Koch ("Exceptional Wretches") writes literary horror and surrealist trash. Their books include *The Wingspan of Severed Hands, Convulsive, Invaginies,* and *The Couvade,* which received a 2019 Shirley Jackson Award nomination. His short works appear in *Nightmare Magazine, Southwest Review, Vastarien, The Mad Butterfly's Ball,* and many others. Find Joe (he/they) at horrorsong.blog.

C.S. Magnuson ("This Place Has Good Roots") is the author of the southern gothic horror novel, *A Light on the Bayou,* as well as the Horror in the Ozarks series which includes *Dark Things Crawl Out,* and *Hidden Children.* Her work has been published in various literary journals including *Space and Time Magazine.* She lives with her family and a horde of unruly canines in Missouri where "Midwest Nice" is always served with a side of Southern spice.

Shane David Morin ("Velvet Bag") is an urban poet living in the Seacoast of New Hampshire. After his second divorce, he had begun writing as a form of grief processing for the parental alienation that accompanied his separation from his daughter. Since then, Shane has honed his craft to blend post-modernity with speculative concepts as well as topics of contemporary horror. Shane holds a passionate fascination with anything space and identifies as a cis-gender male feminist and LGBTQIA++ ally. Shane is currently pursuing an MFA in Poetry at Lasell University. In his spare time, Shane binges *Farscape* and most anything *Star Trek*.

Donna J. W. Munro ("His Edges") teaches high schoolers the slippery truths of government and history at her day job. Her students are her greatest inspiration. She lives with five cats, a cute, curly-haired dog, a fur-covered husband, a sassy septuagenarian mama, and an encyclopedia son. Her daughter is off saving the world.

Donna's pieces are published in *Corvid Queen*, *Enter the Apocalypse*, *It Calls from the Forest*, *Apparition Lit*, *Pseudopod 752*, *Shakespeare Unleashed*, *Novus Monstrum*, *ParABnormal*, and many more. Check out her Poppet Cycle series.

Sumiko Saulson ("A Rise in Red") is a Bram Stoker Award® Finalist for Poetry for *The Rat King* (2022, Dooky Zines) and *Melancholia* (2024, Bludgeoned Girls Press), Elgin Award Nominee (2022), 2018 Afrosurrealist Writers Award, and 2021 Ladies of Horror Readers' Choice Award winner. Their novel *Somnalia: The Metamorphoses of Flynn Keahi* is available from Mocha Memoirs Press

Angela Yuriko Smith, ("Fake Muse") HWA president and *Space and Time* publisher, is a two-time Bram Stoker Award winner. As a Publishing Coach, she helps writers search less and submit more with her weekly calendar of author opportunities at authortunities.substack.com.

Lucy A. Snyder ("Fragility" "The Modern Sisyphus") is the Shirley Jackson Award-nominated and five-time Bram Stoker

Award-winning author of 15 books, 100 published poems, and over 100 published short stories. Her most recent title is the Lovecraftian body horror novel *Sister, Maiden, Monster*. She lives near Columbus, Ohio, with a small jungle of houseplants, a fleet of aquariums, a clowder of cats, a shed of reptiles, and an insomnia of housemates. You can learn more about her at www.lucysnyder.com.

Since 2017, **Valerie B. Williams**' ("Company Policy") short speculative fiction has been published in nearly twenty anthologies and magazines. Highlights include *Space and Time* magazine (April 2025), *Dastardly Damsels* anthology (October 2024), *Dark Corners of the Old Dominion* anthology (September 2023), and *American Gothic Short Stories* anthology (May 2019). Her debut novel, a story of supernatural suspense titled *The Vanishing Twin*, was released in October 2024. She is an Active member of the Horror Writers Association (HWA). Valerie spins twisty tales from her home in central Virginia, which she shares with her very patient husband and equally patient Golden Retriever.

L. Marie Wood ("Vicious") is an International Impact, Golden Stake, and two-time Bookfest Award-winner, as well as an Ignyte and four-time Bram Stoker Award® nominated author. She has won over 50 national and international screenplay and film awards. Wood is also the Vice President of the Horror Writers Association, founder of the Speculative Fiction Academy, an English/Creative Writing professor, and a horror scholar. Learn more at www.lmariewood.com.

DRAGON'S ROOST PRESS

Dragon's Roost Press is the fever dream brainchild of dark speculative fiction author Michael Cieslak. Since 2014, their goal has been to find the best speculative fiction authors and share their work with the public. For more information about Dragon's Roost Press and their publications, please visit:

http://www.thedragonsroost.biz

www.ingramcontent.com/pod-product-compliance
Lightning Source LLC
Chambersburg PA
CBHW060632260626
47161CB00008B/2871